BL=4.3
ARP=5.0

Letting Go of Lisa

You'll want to read these inspiring titles by

Lurlene McDaniel

Angels in Pink
Kathleen's Story • Raina's Story • Holly's Story

One Last Wish Novels
Mourning Song • A Time to Die
Mother, Help Me Live • Someone Dies, Someone Lives
Sixteen and Dying • Let Him Live
The Legacy: Making Wishes Come True • Please Don't Die
She Died Too Young • All the Days of Her Life
A Season for Goodbye • Reach for Tomorrow

Other Fiction
The Time Capsule
Garden of Angels
A Rose for Melinda
Telling Christina Goodbye
How Do I Love Thee: Three Stories
To Live Again
Angel of Mercy
Angel of Hope
Starry, Starry Night: Three Holiday Stories
The Girl Death Left Behind
Angels Watching Over Me
Lifted Up by Angels
Until Angels Close My Eyes
I'll Be Seeing You
Saving Jessica
Don't Die, My Love
Too Young to Die
Goodbye Doesn't Mean Forever
Somewhere Between Life and Death
Time to Let Go
Now I Lay Me Down to Sleep
When Happily Ever After Ends
Baby Alicia Is Dying

From every ending comes a new beginning. . . .

Lurlene McDaniel

Letting Go of Lisa

DELACORTE PRESS

Published by
Delacorte Press
an imprint of
Random House Children's Books
a division of Random House, Inc.
New York

Visit us on the Web! www.randomhouse.com/teens
Educators and librarians, for a variety of teaching tools,
visit us at www.randomhouse.com/teachers

Library of Congress Cataloging-in-Publication Data
McDaniel, Lurlene.
  Letting go of Lisa / Lurlene McDaniel.
    p. cm.
  Summary: Home-schooled for most of his education, Nathan enters
the public high school as a senior where he meets a beautiful girl with a
secret and together they learn about loving, living, and dying.
  ISBN-13: 978-0-385-73159-1 (trade) — ISBN-13: 978-0-385-90196-3 (glb)
  ISBN-10: 0-385-73159-0 (trade) — ISBN-10: 0-385-90196-8 (glb)
[1. Interpersonal relations—Fiction. 2. Grief—Fiction. 3. Cancer—Fic-
tion. 4. Family life—Georgia—Fiction. 5. High schools—Fiction.
6. Schools—Fiction.] I. Title.
PZ7.M13997Let 2006
[Fic]—dc22   2005013215

The text of this book is set in 11-point Adobe Garamond.
Book design by Vikki Sheatsley
Printed in the United States of America

July 2006
BVG   10 9 8 7 6 5 4 3 2 1

Then the angel showed me the river of the water of life, as clear as crystal, flowing from the throne of God and of the Lamb. . . . On each side of the river stood the tree of life, bearing twelve crops of fruit. . . . And the leaves of the tree are for the healing of the nations. Revelation 22:1–2 (NIV)

Letting Go of Lisa

1

The motorcycle cut in front of Nathan Malone just as he was pulling into the high school parking lot. He slammed on the brakes and blasted the car's horn, but the rider on the back, dressed in black leather and a streamlined helmet, flashed him an obscene gesture as the cycle's driver sped off with a roar. Nathan took deep breaths. Another car snaked past him and a voice yelled, "Hey, buddy, park it someplace else! You're jamming traffic."

Startled, Nathan put his foot on the gas and shot forward, almost running over three girls crossing the lot. They shouted at him. He stomped the brake and clamped the wheel, his palms clammy, and inched forward, searching for the parking space assigned to him in his Crestwater welcome packet. His friend Skeet had warned him that the first day was gridlock. Maybe Skeet was used to the bedlam, but Nathan wasn't. Years of homeschooling hadn't prepared him to spend his senior year in one of Atlanta's biggest public high schools, but here he was—ready or not. He shouldn't let the two idiots on the cycle determine his mood.

He found the space, marked by a bright yellow painted number, and pulled in, careful to park between the lines. His car was new—well, not *new* new, but new to him. His parents had given him the keys just a few nights before, part of his seventeenth birthday gift, but also a way to make up for shoving him into a public school from the relative shelter of his homeschooling experience. Not that Nathan minded. He'd wanted to be a regular kid for a long time. And being regular meant attending public school. "A cesspool, my man," Skeet had always said. "Not for the faint of heart."

Nathan shouldered his book bag and headed off for the entrance and the common area, where Skeet had sworn he'd be waiting for him. He'd better be! Nathan already felt tight as a string on his guitar, and that was *before* the incident with the cycle.

The halls were packed and so noisy Nathan wanted to cover his ears. How did people *think,* much less *study,* in this decibel purgatory? One good thing about his home classroom—it was quiet. Or it had been quiet until the twins, Abby and Audrey, were born in July and his mother realized in a panic that she couldn't juggle two babies *and* teach Nathan's senior class load. Not with college looming. At first he'd felt euphoric, like he'd been let out of a cage, but now, in the teeming hallways, he felt dwarfed and lost. What every other kid in the school knew as normal, he saw as extraordinary.

"Nate!" Skeet's voice cut through the noise. "Over here!"

Nathan worked his way over to Skeet, who was sitting on a short wall. The wall surrounded a monolith of concrete and brass: Crestwater's mascot, a rising dolphin balancing on its tail. "Hey, man."

"Find your space?"

"Yeah. But not before a cycle almost plowed me down. Aren't they illegal on school property?"

"Not so." His brow puckered. "Who was driving?"

"How should I know? There were two of them. The rider on the back gave me the finger when I honked."

Skeet grinned. "Odds are it was Lisa Lindstrom."

"A *girl*?" Most of the girls Nathan knew were home-schooled like him, younger, all giggly and silly, and they didn't ride cycles and flash rude hand gestures.

"Was the cycle black and silver with a big red heart painted on the tank?"

"I didn't take that close a look. It almost creamed me. I was just trying to get out of the way."

"Not a guy in the school who wouldn't give up his car speakers to get a tumble from Lisa. She's a knockout—transferred in as a junior last January. Keeps to herself, though. I call her 'a heartache on a Harley.' " Skeet pressed his hand over his heart.

"She sounds like a conceited pain."

"No . . . she just doesn't give a damn. I know, hard to believe, but she seems to be totally unimpressed by Crestwater's movers and shakers. She's my hero." Skeet leaned closer. "She's the one who stood up Rod Stewart for the junior-senior last year."

Nathan put the pieces together. Rod "Roddy" Stewart, no relation to the rocker, was a football legend at Crestwater and on track for a full ride to Georgia and the Bulldogs after he graduated. Skeet had told Nathan all about the big dump the day after last year's prom because it was all over the school and because Skeet didn't like Roddy. "*That* was the girl?"

"Way the story goes, Rod went to pick her up and she was long gone—off to a frat party, according to her mother, who said, 'Gee, you're the second boy tonight who showed up to take her to the prom.'" Skeet cackled gleefully. "Seems she jilted some other poor punk too. We never did know who. Man, Roddy was steamed. I mean, who stands up Mr. 'I'm Too Sexy for My Shorts' and lives to tell about it?"

"Well, she still doesn't sound like the kind of girl a guy gets all warm and fuzzy over."

"You got that right. She's—" He searched for words. "The stuff legends are made of."

Nathan laughed. "You sound like you're in love with her."

Skeet looked self-conscious. "I'm not in her league. Besides, you haven't seen the biker dude up close who sometimes rides with her. He could squash your head with his bare hands."

"Okay, okay. Let's move on." He dug out his class schedule. He was in all AP classes, nothing with Skeet. "Meet me here at the end of the day and I'll drive us home."

"Football rally after school on the field. We've got to go and drool over the cheerleaders."

"Oh." Nathan disliked that he was so out of sync with high school life that he didn't know the basics. "I thought you hated football."

"I *hate* Rod. There's a difference. Come to the rally with me, then we'll head home."

"I'll have to call Mom. You know how she freaks when I'm late."

Suddenly Skeet's eyes widened. "Here she comes," he said under his breath.

Nathan turned to see a tall girl with long chestnut-colored hair striding past. She wore black leather pants, cowboy boots, and a trendy top. She carried a black leather jacket over her shoulder. "The diva?" he asked out of the side of his mouth.

"In the flesh," Skeet said reverently.

Nathan eyed her. Skeet had been right about her being pretty. Yet everything about her body language said *Stay away.* A group of girls stepped aside when Lisa passed. A few of them giggled, and others started whispering. She ignored them.

"You're staring. I thought you were mad at her," Skeet teased after Lisa had gone.

Nathan reddened. "Pretty doesn't make up for everything."

The first bell buzzed. Skeet scooped up his backpack. "Time to begin our jail sentences. Catch you here after last period."

Nathan turned and confidently headed to the stairs and his first period. He had come by the week before and followed his daily schedule from room to room just so he wouldn't get lost and wander around like a ninth-grade newbie. He was the first one in the room and the teacher looked up, surprised. Nathan nodded and slid into a seat in a middle row, realizing that being early to class was not a badge of honor. At home, his mother started his lessons with great punctuality, making the case that it was insulting to keep others waiting. He shuffled through his notebook self-consciously as others trickled into the room, eyeing him suspiciously.

By lunchtime, Nathan had been stepped on, pushed, elbowed, splattered from a drinking fountain, and called an ugly name for encroaching on someone else's perceived space. He took his tray outside into the courtyard, found a spot under a tree and ate alone. Everyone else seemed to be huddled into groups, eating and laughing together. He was the odd man out, friendless and nameless to others who'd gone to school together for years. He'd been placed in all accelerated classes because of test scores, and so far, his classroom work hadn't sounded difficult. In fact, the classroom lectures had been painfully slow and shallow, so unlike his homeschooling, which had allowed him to master subjects at his own pace. He had to hand it to his mother. She'd been a good teacher.

He recalled the worried look on her face that morning as she juggled his twin sisters, one in each arm. "I'm sorry I have to feed you to the wolves, Nathan."

His father looked up from the paper. "Don't be dramatic, Karen. He's going to public school, not an internment camp."

"Crestwater had a drug bust last year. I *hate* sending him there."

Nathan looked up from his plate of scrambled eggs. "It's all right, Mom. I'm okay about it." Not that his parents hadn't tried to get him into a good private school, but by the time his mother had realized she'd have to bail on teaching him, none of the area's private schools had any slots for seniors.

"We've agreed," Craig Malone said, sounding weary. "Crestwater's close. He has a car. His best friend goes there. It's only for one year. Can we move on?"

Nathan hated it when his parents talked about him while he was right in front of them. Was he transparent? Fortunately one of the twins started crying, so his mother left the kitchen to nurse her.

"She'll adjust," his dad said good-naturedly. "Her family's everything. You know that."

Nathan did know that. Automatically his gaze shifted to the front of the refrigerator. It was coated with magnets holding photos, memos, drawings—and one in particular that claimed center stage, a frayed, yellowed piece of art paper of a child's drawing showing a house, a family of four holding hands, a sun in a blue sky, green grass and a tree. *Molly's last drawing.*

Nathan snapped from his reverie when a group of laughing girls sauntered past the tree where he sat. Once they passed, he stood, dusted off his jeans and lugged his trash back inside the cafeteria. The smell of stale food assailed his nose. His last class of the day, Advanced World Lit and Creative Writing, was the one he was looking forward to most. He loved to write, and he'd been told by Skeet that the teacher, Max Fuller, had a rep for being tough but excellent.

Nathan wasn't disappointed by Fuller's classroom. Bookshelves were stuffed with volumes of books, the teacher's desk was shoved into a far corner, and a lectern stood in the center of a double semicircle. Fuller himself looked rumpled in a well-worn suit jacket and polo shirt. Nathan grabbed a seat in the second circle, directly in front of the lectern, and watched as the room slowly filled. He counted twenty-two other students—the smallest number of all his classes. Only the student desk directly in front of him remained unoccupied; then, just after the bell sounded, a girl strolled in.

Nathan's heart skipped a beat as he recognized the black leather pants and cascade of chestnut hair.

"Nice of you to join us, Miss Lindstrom," Fuller said in a gravelly voice. "This seat's for you." He pointed to the one in front of Nathan. She slipped into the vacant chair and her long thick hair brushed Nathan's desktop. He caught a whiff of fresh rain and musk and swallowed hard. His palms went clammy, his mouth dry. How was he going to get through a whole year with the scent of such a wicked angel hovering around him like an enchanted mist?

$\mathcal{A}$ ll the way to the commons, Nathan pictured the expression on Skeet's face when he'd tell him about having a class with the Harley Princess. When he arrived in the area, Skeet was huddled in a corner, his arms crossed, the collar of his shirt turned up as if to hide his face. "Hey, man, shouldn't we be heading out to the rally?"

"I'm not going."

"What? This morning you said—"

"You go without me."

Nathan could see that Skeet was really upset. He waited until the area cleared of foot traffic before he asked, "What happened?"

Skeet looked up, his eyes hooded. "Nothing happened. I changed my mind. I don't want to go."

"If you're not going, neither am I." Nathan swung his book bag over his shoulder. "Come on. Let's go home."

Skeet slowly rose, picked up his book bag and followed Nathan to the parking lot. From the direction of the football field, Nathan heard the sounds of the marching band and of kids cheering. He drove slowly, taking backstreets toward their neighborhood. "Want to stop at my place first?" Nathan asked. "You'll be doing me a favor by putting off the third degree Mom will be giving me."

Skeet shrugged. "Cookies and milk?"

"You know her too well. She probably baked all afternoon."

"At least she's home."

Another sore spot in Skeet's life: a cold mother whose job was more important than raising a kid, and a stepfather who was downright mean to Skeet. Skeet's parents used to lock him out on weekends, rain or shine, and Nathan's family would take him in like a stray puppy. Over time, the boys became friends and discovered their mutual love of country music; they formed a garage-band duo in ninth grade. Skeet often said, "We'll take over Nashville."

"Except that neither of us can sing," Nathan would remind him.

"Singers will beg to join us," Skeet usually replied, pounding his keyboard.

"So, are your classes doable?" Nathan asked, making conversation.

"I guess."

"No good news to report?"

"No." Skeet was hunkered down in the seat, staring glumly at the dashboard. After a few minutes of silence, he said, "Why do you suppose they stick a guy like me into last period phys ed?"

"Don't know." Nathan had the class right before lunch.

"Well, Winston George Andrews got assigned to last period. You know, the period with all the football jocks."

Nathan's heart sank. "Probably a computer glitch. You can get it changed."

"Sure. Whiny-boy asks to get moved away from the big bad jocks."

Nathan waited patiently for Skeet to tell his story.

"Rod and his thugs shoved me into the hall in my Skivvies just before the bell rang. I was all but naked and every girl on the cheerleading squad was passing by. Of course, it was a big joke. Ha-ha."

Nathan felt the sting of his friend's humiliation. "Did you tell the coach?"

"Get off it, Nate. The nerds don't go tattling on the big bad football boys who can do no wrong because they can catch a ball while running."

"Well, it isn't fair."

"What is *fair* in life?"

"I could write a song about it."

"What would you call it?"

"How about, 'I Caught Your Heart While Chasing After Pigskin Blues.' "

For the first time, Skeet smiled. "Sounds demented."

Nathan pulled into his driveway. "Come on in. Be quiet in case the twins are asleep."

"Can you tell them apart yet?" Skeet followed Nathan through the garage and into the kitchen, warm and smelling of chocolate and cinnamon.

"Nope. They're exactly alike—both screamers." Nathan scooped up cookies cooling on a wire rack and grabbed a gallon of milk from the fridge. "Glasses," he said over his shoulder. Skeet took two from a cabinet and followed him into the basement. It was decorated like a bistro, with a small table, a coffee bar, two sofas, bean bags and a giant-screen television.

"How was your first day?" Skeet asked when they'd poured milk and settled into bean bags. "Think you can get the hang of high school?"

"A couple of teachers almost put me to sleep. The best class is my last, lit. Fuller's going to be tough, but I like him. We have to turn in a creative piece this Friday and then every third Friday until the year's over. He assigned us all secret numbers. On Monday, he's going to read the best of the submissions, but only by their special number. That way, no one will know who wrote the piece, but we'll all get to hear what he thinks is good work." Nathan shoved a cookie in his mouth. "And I plan to write the piece he reads first. Number seven-oh-five. You heard it here."

"I can't wait to see the movie."

"Well, here's something else to eat your heart out over. Guess who's sitting right in front of me in Fuller's class?"

"Impress me."

"Lisa, the Harley Princess."

"You lie!"

Nathan grinned. "Scout's honor."

"Talk about unfair! I get creepy football jocks and you get a goddess. She sits right in front of you?"

"Her hair's so long that it almost touches my desk."

"You're going to fall madly in love with her. Wait and see."

"No way."

Skeet pointed his finger at Nathan in an imitation of firing a gun. "Pow. Dead meat at Lisa's feet."

Nathan was spared the third degree about his school day until the dinner table that night. His mother peppered him with questions, and he tried to answer politely, but it seemed to him that his interior space was being grossly invaded. Yes, he could handle the coursework. Yes, it was an adjustment listening to someone drone on in a lecture. No, he never got lost. Sure, he had met some "good" kids—not exactly true, but it was what she wanted to hear.

Finally his father interjected. "We miss you down at the firm. The gang says hi."

One of the perks of homeschooling was that

Nathan had been able to work downtown at his dad's place of employment, a large architectural and engineering firm. He had worked there two full summers and sometimes during the workweek when his homeschooling load was light. "Tell them I'll be back over Christmas holidays."

His father nodded, took another slice of meat. "I hope we have extra jobs at Christmas. Business is slow."

"I can get another job. The malls are always needing extra help for holidays."

"You don't have to work at all," his mother said. "This is your last year at home. Maybe you could just hang around."

Nathan looked at her as if she'd grown another head. "I'd be bored to death."

"Would that be so horrible? A little boredom? Besides, you don't really know how difficult school will be. And the twins should get to know their big brother."

"They're babies, Mom. All they do is eat, sleep and poop."

"They won't always be little."

"Karen, leave the kid alone. If he wants to work, he should. A little extra money for college isn't a bad thing."

Nathan sighed. They were talking around him again, as if he'd suddenly gone transparent. He stood up from the table. "I'm going to get a jump start on some assignments." He went straight down to the basement and through the special door, into a room set aside for his homeschooling.

His mother had transformed the space into a classroom that changed with him over the years. There was table space to work, a computer hooked to the Internet, bookshelves, a blackboard, and even a small area with test tubes where they'd worked on chemistry the year before. He'd gone on field trips once a month with other homeschoolers, and when he was younger, he'd played in a soccer league. He'd dropped out of everything in tenth grade. Deep inside, he longed for something he could never put into words. He wanted to touch and taste and feel anything that would shake his small, protected world and help him express the fire that burned inside him. Music came close. He was certain there was more, something he hadn't yet come across, but it *had* to be out there. Waiting. Nathan felt stifled and hemmed in, like an animal in too small of a cage.

He sat down at the computer and opened the writing program, intent on starting his piece for Fuller's class. He wanted it to be good enough to be selected for the first reading. Without warning, the screen blurred and a vision of Lisa's hair tumbling down her back filled his thoughts. He'd wanted to grab a handful and bury his face in it.

He'd been attracted to a few girls over the years, homeschoolers like himself, but he'd been too shy to act on those feelings and they'd passed quickly. This girl was different. She was a loner too. This girl intrigued him.

He touched the keyboard and willed his brain to concentrate on his assignment. Lisa was competition. He had no idea if she could write; told himself that she was probably as deep as the fluff on a dandelion. Her badass attitude was probably a cover for what *wasn't* inside. According to Skeet, everyone in high school had an image to uphold, a personal facade. Lisa Lindstrom was no different. Nathan just had to crack it open. He was sure that once he did, he would forget all about her.

3

By Friday, Nathan was nursing a huge case of jitters. Not just because of the assignment, which he'd worked on harder than anything he'd ever turned in to his mother, but also because he couldn't seem to get into the rhythm of Crestwater High. The constant noise bothered him still. Even in classrooms when it was supposed to be quiet, kids coughed, shuffled, whispered. The teachers' lectures moved at a snail's pace. Entire days passed in slow motion. Plus, his senses had become finely attuned to Lisa's every movement.

"I don't think that's her boyfriend on the Harley," he told Skeet on Friday morning as they walked in from the parking lot.

"And why do you think that, Sherlock?"

"He slows, she jumps off, grabs her stuff and walks

away. No kisses goodbye. No tonsil exploration. Is that SOP around here?"

"The tongue tangles?" Skeet shrugged. "Yeah, pretty much. But only if you're related."

"Funny." Nathan jerked open his locker without smiling. "Whatever happened to modesty?"

"What's yanking your chain today?"

"I turn in that assignment for Fuller. Guess it's got me spooked."

"Is it that important to you that he plucks your paper from the pile? I mean, *why*? Sounds like you'll get another shot at it between now and graduation."

"I just want to be the *first* best paper. Hard to explain."

Skeet looked baffled, then shrugged again. "Whatever, dude."

Nathan shut his locker. "Did you work out your phys ed problem?"

"I signed up for the tennis team. They meet last period too."

"You don't play tennis."

"Our little secret. It beats facing Roddy and his gang every day. Two cute girls on the team though. Course, they can pound me into the asphalt in the game, but I'll be alive. Besides, how bad can a sport be with the word *love* in it?"

Nathan grinned, feeling guilty that he hadn't helped Skeet solve his problem with the jocks. "Want to knock a few balls around tomorrow? It's been a while and I'm not good, but you'll get some practice in."

"Hey, that would be cool." Skeet flashed a grateful smile as the first bell sounded. "I work the early shift at the store, so I'll be off by three o'clock." He bagged groceries for spending money—and to stay out of his house as much as possible.

Nathan sprinted off, rounded a corner and ran smack into Lisa Lindstrom. He grabbed her arm to steady her. "Wow, sorry!"

She twisted away as if he'd burned her. "Hands off."

He stepped back. "I—I didn't mean . . ."

Her eyes narrowed. "Are you blushing?"

Nathan's neck and cheeks felt hot. "No!"

"It sure looks like you are."

Their gazes locked and he was startled to see that her eyes were blue-violet. He'd never seen eyes that color before. "Is blushing a crime?"

"No crime," she said quietly. "Sort of refreshing, really."

"Well golly, gee whiz, I'll have to remember to do it more often."

Her expression hardened. "Don't bother. The charm is gone."

She turned and he felt a second of panic. He had been talking to her and now he'd put her off with a smart-aleck remark. Bad move. He caught up with her in a couple of strides. "Didn't mean to sound sarcastic. Sorry."

She stopped again. "You sit behind me in Fuller's class, don't you."

"Guilty as charged. Nathan Malone, which is Gaelic for 'he who blushes freely.' "

She suppressed a smile, making his heart beat faster. If he could keep her talking . . . "Um—you got your assignment?"

"I always have my assignments for his class. He's the only teacher in this place worth his paycheck."

"Really?"

"He was teaching college and stepped down to high school because college freshmen were so ill prepared. He figured he'd better come back to the source and do the job right. Plenty of people want to take his class, but only a few make it in."

"How does one make it in?"

"Test scores and ability to write. How do you not know that? Are you new? Living under a rock?"

"Yes to both questions. I've been homeschooled up until now." She studied him with an intensity that made his mouth go dry. He added, "Ever since sixth grade."

"Six years of homeschooling?"

"My mom has a degree in education, so she's good at it."

He willed her to ask more questions, but the tardy bell buzzed.

"You're late to class," she said. "You'll get a black mark." She turned, headed into a girls' bathroom.

"You're late too," he called. "Won't you get a tardy?"

"The difference between us, Malone, is that *I* don't care."

"I don't care either," he called as she disappeared into the bathroom.

"Liar!" he heard her say through the door.

And she was right. Nathan didn't want any black marks on his record. He didn't want to have to return to being homeschooled. From this moment on, he had one goal: to look into Lisa Lindstrom's blue-violet eyes every day for the rest of the year.

When Nathan walked into Fuller's class, Lisa was nowhere around. He wondered if she had skipped the whole day. He didn't have time to dwell on it because the first thing Fuller did was take up the writing assignments, and then announce that they were going to begin a study of nineteenth- and early twentieth-century poets. "Because I know all of you have read *Beowulf* and Shakespeare until you're sick to death of them," he said. His gravelly voice dripped sarcasm.

Actually, Nathan had read those works, but he wouldn't have admitted it publicly. Too nerdy, even for an advanced class. He fought to concentrate the whole fifty minutes, but his thoughts kept drifting to Lisa. Where was she? Why hadn't she shown up, or turned in her assignment after telling him that she never missed turning them in? Fuller's class only admitted top students, and it was a class she'd said she liked. Nathan was forced to assume that she really *didn't* care. What he couldn't figure out was why.

After school, he dropped off Skeet at the grocery store where he worked and drove home. His mother wasn't inside, and when he peeked into the nursery, the

twins were sound asleep. He grabbed a bag of chips and strolled into the backyard, where he found her in her grubby gardening clothes planting a bush.

"How was your day?" she asked.

"Fine. Isn't it early to be planting the beds?" He knew she planted annuals twice a year, but the summer begonias still looked bright and healthy, and the weather hadn't turned cool enough to plant pansies. He knew because her large well-groomed gardens were expertly tended despite the birth of the babies, and because he helped her keep them that way.

"The nursery had only a few pink camellia bushes, so I had to buy one before they were gone." She shoveled aside a scoop of red Georgia clay.

Suddenly Nathan remembered. It was September, and she always planted something special and showy in September. "So that's what you picked out this year—a camellia?" he asked, catching himself, hoping she hadn't noticed he'd forgotten the date.

She leaned on the shovel, exertion showing on her face. "It's a new variety. Pale pink that darkens as it opens. And it's all right, Nate. I don't expect you to remember the way I do."

Her voice was kind, but still he felt bad. "I—I can help dig the hole."

"No. I like digging the hole." A shadow crossed her face. "It's therapeutic, you know."

He wanted to say, *But Mom, it's been fourteen years.* Instead, he said, "Well, if you change your mind."

"Just listen for the twins to wake up. It's close to another feeding time." She wiped her brow, smearing a swatch of red soil across her forehead. "Of course, it's *always* close to a feeding time these days."

Nathan smiled because he knew that's what she needed him to do. Which was one of the basic problems he found about being homeschooled—they knew each other too well. Nathan jogged back to the house, grateful that she had Abby and Audrey now. It would make it easier for him when it came his time to leave next year. At least, he hoped it would, because he wasn't living at home while attending college like she wanted. He was determined to move, no matter how difficult the uprooting.

4

*C*ertain that boredom was going to make him go crazy, Nathan busied himself over the weekend with chores and playing guitar. He knocked the tennis ball around with Skeet on the public courts, and took a hard whack in the side when he heard the sound of a motorcycle and looked over to the road in anticipation that it might be Lisa. It wasn't. The only truly bad thing that happened was when Skeet came over Sunday evening sporting a bright red handprint on the side of his face.

"What happened?" Nathan asked, knowing the answer already.

"My old man said I smarted off to him."

"Want to stay the night?"

Skeet shook his head. "I'll just wait until he has a few beers and falls asleep. I'll clear out before he's even up in the morning."

"Come have breakfast."

"Your mom still cook those big feasts?" Skeet had come over many times for a hot breakfast when he was younger and locked outside.

"What can I say? Supermom lives right here in Atlanta."

"I'll be here." Skeet picked up the game controller from the coffee table and punched up one of Nathan's video games. "Got time to play one?"

"Sure."

They sat in concentrated silence until long after Nathan's parents had turned off the lights upstairs and gone to bed, the steady action of the game taking both of them out of their real worlds and into another world, more adventurous and, for Skeet, far safer.

On Monday morning, Nathan watched Lisa dismount her cycle and the driver speed off. She hoisted her backpack and headed toward the building, passing a group of ballplayers on the way. They made kissing sounds that she ignored, flashed them the finger when they made remarks Nathan couldn't hear. He wondered if she'd show up to Fuller's class since she hadn't handed in an assignment on Friday. Fuller had made it very clear that if the assignments weren't handed in on time, he wouldn't accept them at all, and since the work counted for a third of each student's grade, it was in a student's best interest to hand them in on time.

Lisa did show for the class, and Nathan nodded at

her when he caught her eye. She took her seat and he was left to stare at her thick chestnut hair laced with the scent of fresh oranges—*like a Creamsicle,* he thought.

Standing at his podium, Fuller said, "The first business of the day is to read the best paper turned in on Friday." He flipped open a manila folder and Nathan's mouth went dry. Would the piece be his? He had thought it the best creative writing he'd ever done, an essay about the role of music in everyday life.

"Let me begin by saying that most of you did very ordinary writing—a situation I hope to correct as we are immersed in good writing by great masters and thinkers from the past. Only one standout in this first bunch."

Nathan's heart thudded. Fuller leaned over the podium. "The writer is number four-five-four." Nathan's heart sank. "The piece is a free-form poem titled 'Wings to Fly.'" Nathan slumped in his chair and Fuller began to read:

> *I have fashioned wings of wax and feathers and*
> *   carefully formed them as things of beauty.*
> *   And utility.*
> *Snow white.*
> *Pale yellow.*
> *They glow like cat's eyes.*
> *And I have tied the wings to my thin, earthbound*
> *   arms, and found a place*
> *on a high rock from which to hurl*
> *   myself.*

I'll pass just above the sea, being careful not to let
*   the feathers drench.*
I'll pass low away from the sun and suddenly I am
*   flying, flying.*
And I wait for night to fall so that I can fly higher.
Suddenly this space is too safe.
And night will come too dark.
For if I only fly and do not soar, how will I know
*   the universe*
How will I know what lies inside. Of me?
For starlight is pale and far away.
Stars prick darkness but are not warm.
And so I choose to soar. Upward into blue-lit sky
*   and closer to the sun until I feel the wax*
*   dripping, melting, trickling into the sea of*
*   glass-still water.*
And yet, unafraid, I fly straight toward the sun.
Straight toward the Son.
Will I be caught?
Or will I melt into the sea below?

Fuller looked up at the hushed classroom, his expression intense. He walked to the blackboard and wrote the final few lines for them to see. Nathan was struck by the different spellings of *sun/Son,* each with a different meaning, and by the imagery that linked them.

Fuller continued. "I leave each of you to ponder the mind-set of this writer and to glean the message there for all of us." He returned to his podium, tucked the paper into the folder. Nathan yearned to hear this teacher read one of his pieces with such reverence. "And please note, there wasn't a four-letter word in the piece. Ladies and gentlemen, English is an amazing language, full of both plentiful and beautiful words. Several of you peppered your work with four-letter words. Why? Shock value? Do you think I don't know these words? Frankly, I think using them shows weakness of mind and lack of talent. Stretch yourselves, writers. Make me *care* about your pubescent thoughts in poetic language, not gutter-speak."

Students shuffled feet and shifted at their desks. Nathan cut his eyes sideways on the chance that the writer might subtly reveal himself with a look of pride or embarrassment or satisfaction, but all expressions were merely curious.

When the class was over, Nathan scooped up his books, walked quickly to catch up with Lisa in the crowded halls. "How are you doing?" he asked, falling in step beside her. She looked at him, startled. Did no one even dare speak to the Great Lisa?

"Why do you ask?"

Her question caught him off guard. Usually people said, "Fine" or "Life sucks" or anything other than "Why do you ask." He said, "I mean, you weren't in class Friday. I thought maybe something happened."

"Are you my social secretary, Malone?"

At least she remembered his name. "You said you liked

Fuller's class, but you didn't show. I thought maybe something went wrong. It's an inquiry, not an inquisition."

"I had an appointment," she said quickly. "Nothing sinister."

After an awkward moment, he asked, "So, who do you think writer four-five-four is?"

"Was it yours?"

"I wish."

"It was okay," she said with a shrug.

"The reference to classical mythology was a nice touch. And the use of *sun* with two meanings was pretty cool."

She stopped and foot traffic flowed around them. "You read mythology, Malone? Or did you pick it up from Saturday morning cartoons?"

He felt color seep into his neck at her put-down. He didn't understand why she was being so caustic and unfriendly. "I've read a lot of the old Greek and Roman stories. And I thought the poem Fuller read was deep. Didn't you?" He held her gaze like a firebrand, determined not to let her get away with it.

She blinked, turned. "I like mythology too. Not sure if I liked the poem. I've got to go."

He stepped in front of her. "Homeschooling isn't a free ride, you know. I had to work hard and pass regular performance tests. I think public school—this school—is a cakewalk. Kids don't seem like they care much about their classes, and most of them can't carry on a conversation beyond next week's football game or who's dating whom."

She didn't respond right away, but he could tell he'd

gotten her attention. "Don't think that I feel like home-schooling is inferior to this, because I don't." She sounded apologetic. "I think you're lucky to have been able to be homeschooled. It implies somebody cares for you."

"Are you saying nobody cares for you?"

The halls were almost empty now and she took a few steps backward toward the outside door. "Wrong assumption, Malone."

It had been a stupid thing for him to ask. Of course somebody cared about her. She probably had a hundred somebodies who cared about her. He screwed up his courage. "Want to talk about it over coffee sometime? I can call you."

"A date?" she asked.

"Why not? Pick a time and place."

"I don't date."

He watched her step through the doorway into the bright afternoon sunlight. The motorcycle was waiting, and this time Nathan saw the driver more clearly: a lanky man with muscular arms and chest, work boots and dirty jeans. He wore a dark helmet and his long hair stuck out from under it. He handed Lisa a helmet and she slung her leg over the Harley's seat, slipped her book bag onto her back. The man gunned the motor, kicked off from the curb. Nathan watched the cycle speed away.

Nathan told Skeet all that had happened on the ride home. Skeet listened and didn't remind him about his prediction that Nathan would tumble for Lisa. "Takes courage to ask, man."

"I don't believe she doesn't date," Nathan grumbled.

"Hey, here's something to cheer you up. Crestwater's playing Highland Friday night, and Highland's better. Which means that Roddy has a good chance of getting his butt kicked. Want to come watch with me?"

"Why not." Nathan's disdain for the jocks had grown over the past few days. They really did act as if they were a superior breed when he knew they weren't. Rumor was that two had paid underclassmen to write papers for them, and if their teachers knew about it, they let it slide.

"And"—Skeet drummed on the dashboard— "rumor is there's going to be a party after. Location to be revealed."

An illegal party. Nathan knew his parents would never let him go. But then, why should he have to tell them? He was perfectly capable of attending a party without getting into trouble. It was about time that he struck out on his own, blew off steam and had some fun.

5

*L*isa Lindstrom was unable to pinpoint the exact moment Nathan Malone came on her radar; she just knew that she slowly became aware of him, like a buzz one starts to hear in a quiet room. One minute all is silent, then a sound begins to break through a person's subconscious and annoys until the person has to stop what she's doing and go find the source. She tried to ignore him, this noise, but one day he broke through—she looked up and saw the most incredible blue eyes, fringed with thick dark lashes, staring at her. Nathan's eyes.

She determined to steer clear, keep him at arm's length as she did so many others, which would have been easier if she hadn't sensed intelligence and sensitivity behind his eyes. Why couldn't he be self-absorbed like Roddy and his jock friends? Or shy? Or avant garde and far out like the goths? Instead he was lean, dark-haired and blue-eyed—an apparition sent to bedevil her when she had no time for it.

"Is that the guy?" Charlie Terry asked Friday afternoon when Lisa climbed onto the back of the cycle.

"What guy?"

"The one staring at you from the doorway."

Lisa disliked the teasing tone in Charlie's voice. "I should have kept my mouth shut and never mentioned him to you."

"Why? I'm in favor of you finding somebody good enough for you."

"Sorry. It's not on my to-do list." Lisa shoved on a helmet, fastened the chin strap.

"It should be."

"Well, it isn't."

"You're being stubborn, Lisa."

"My life. My choice." Charlie was dirty from the construction site where he worked, but she wrapped her arms around his chest anyway. "We leaving or sitting here all day?"

Charlie gunned the engine and kicked off from the curb.

By the start of the fourth quarter, it was evident that Highland was the better football team. Crestwater's cheerleaders attempted to whip up the crowd, but enthusiasm was low. "Go team!" Skeet shouted.

Only Nathan knew his friend was cheering for the other team. "Your school spirit is awesome."

"Ain't it, though?" Skeet grinned, watching Roddy limp to the sidelines between two coaches. "Oo-o-o. Did the big mean tackle hurt you, Roddy?"

"I don't think he can hear you."

"And I don't want him to either." Skeet grinned again. "I'm going to grab a soda before they close the concession stand. Want anything?"

"I'm good." Nathan watched Skeet pick his way down the bleachers. The crowd was beginning to thin, leaving the dismal game despite the cheerleaders' frenzied shouting. Nathan's gaze stopped cold on Lisa. She was sitting below him and to the far left beside a heavyset short-haired girl. His view of her had been blocked by others. Nathan was almost at the top of the bleachers, and he could see the parking lot. With cars pulling out, it was easier to distinguish the layout, and off to one side, he saw her Harley. It gleamed black and silver when headlights struck it. He didn't see her "driver," so that probably meant she'd ridden it to the game herself.

Nathan's heart beat faster. Should he go down and accidentally bump into her? What would he say? He weighed his options, but before he could act, Skeet was back and Nathan decided to do nothing. He didn't want to drag Skeet with him and risk a rebuff.

"I got a party update," Skeet said. He pulled out a napkin with a crude map drawn on it. "It's near Lake

Lanier. Some kid's grandfather owns land out there and it's very private."

"That's pretty far out. You sure you want to go?" Nathan was having second thoughts. He'd told his parents there was a school dance after the game and they'd extended his curfew until twelve-thirty. He hadn't liked lying to them, especially to his mother, because she was so scared for him when he was out of her sight.

"Come on," Skeet said as Highland made another touchdown. "We have to celebrate Highland's victory some way or another."

By the time they arrived at the designated farmland site, the party was in full swing. Cars were parked haphazardly on wet grass and a large bonfire danced in a fire pit. Kids swarmed around the crackling flames and among coolers full of beer and wine drinks. Music boomed from a portable amp hooked to a generator. Couples had already paired off and were dancing or slipping away into the darkness with blankets.

"Does this guy's grandfather know about this?" Nathan asked.

"I doubt it. But we'll be long gone by the time he hears about it. Smell that sweet air?" Skeet asked. "Weed. Want some? It'll cost a few bucks."

"No, and neither do you." Nathan struggled with his conscience. On the one hand, he felt daring and bold; on the other, guilty. He shouldn't even be here. What so many of the kids took as their regular rites, Nathan had never done. He'd spent a lifetime pinned in place by his parents, and now he was a social retard—even by Skeet's standards, who was hardly a party animal.

Skeet had no chance to argue his case for a joint because the sound of a cycle reverberated in the already noisy night air. Nathan turned and saw Lisa on her Harley. His mouth went dry. Skeet said, "I never expected her to show."

"Wasn't she invited?"

"Dude, no one here was invited. Word went around and whoever wanted to come, did." Skeet looked thoughtful. "It's just that she doesn't party with us high school dweebs."

"Well, she's here."

Skeet's eyes narrowed. "You aren't thinking that you're going to get her to look your way, are you?"

"No," Nathan said hastily, although it was exactly what he was thinking. "I was just making an observation."

Skeet rocked back on his heels. "Listen, I'm going to go get a beer. Want one? Or should I bring you a bottle of spring water?"

Nathan didn't really like beer—he'd tasted it on the sly at certain homeschool parties—but he didn't like the way Skeet was riding him either. "Bring me a beer," he said as Skeet walked away.

He kept an eye on Lisa as she tied her helmet to the cycle. He waved. She saw him, gave a halfhearted wave in return, but it was all he needed to hustle over to her side. He said, "I saw you at the game with some girl."

"Jodie Price. She's a friend."

"She didn't come with you to the party?"

"Jodie didn't want to come. She hates crowds." A damp chill had fallen on the field, and fog hovered just above the grass in the distance. Lisa watched several of the cheerleaders clumped together around the fire. "Not all girls travel in packs," she added.

"Why *did* you come?"

"Haven't you heard? I'm a party girl."

The two images he had of Lisa, one of a party princess and the other of a loner, didn't mesh. He was about to tell her that when a voice shouted, "Fight!"

Kids rushed toward the bonfire. Nathan and Lisa went to see what was happening. In the middle of the semicircle formed around the fire and the beer stash, Skeet was standing between Roddy and two of his fellow players. The three of them held bottles of beer and looked roaring drunk and as big as tanks. Roddy was in Skeet's face, which looked pale but stony in the firelight. Roddy gave Skeet a shove. "Who invited you, faggot?"

Skeet said nothing, and that only seemed to make Roddy madder.

Nathan shouldered his way through the crowd and broke into the open. "Hey, leave him alone."

Roddy looked up, and Nathan saw that the side of his face was swollen and that his eye was turning black—hits from the game, Nathan assumed. "Who're you? A fellow faggot?" For some reason, this made a few in the crowd laugh.

Nathan stood beside Skeet. "I'm his friend." He was scared, but Roddy's rattlesnake meanness made Nathan mad. "He's not doing anything to you."

"He's breathing my air."

Again, laughter.

"Then let me remove him from your illustrious presence."

Nathan's sarcasm wasn't lost on Roddy, who cursed him. He leaned into Nathan's face. "I'm going to kick your ass first."

"How about mine, Roddy? Going to kick mine too?" The voice was Lisa's, and the crowd parted and started buzzing as she stepped into the circle next to Nathan and Skeet.

Roddy swayed and called her a skank.

"Hey!" Nathan said. "You can't talk like that to her."

"Says who? You with her, faggot-boy?"

"Nobody's with me," Lisa said. Firelight flickered over her face, reflecting in her eyes, now dark as the night sky. "But if you touch any of us, it won't look too good on the police report," she said. "You know, the one I'll file and that will go on your permanent record for the Georgia coach to read when he's considering you for scholarship money."

Nathan could hardly believe her bravado. Roddy was hateful when he was sober, downright venomous when he was drunk.

Roddy's expression twisted, but he didn't take a swing at any of them. Nathan held his breath. Rod's two buddies grabbed his arms. "Come on," one said. "They ain't worth it."

Roddy swore some more, tossed what was left of his beer at Skeet and Nathan, and swaggered off. The crowd gave the three football players a wide path, mumbling among themselves, then turned away. Skeet wiped beer from his cheek with his sleeve. "He could have killed us."

Nathan's knees felt wobbly, but he didn't let on. "He's a jerk—" he started.

The night was split by the wail of sirens. Somebody screamed, "Cops!" and the kids scattered like roaches across the field toward their cars.

"No, firetrucks!" another voice amended, but no one was listening.

Skeet pulled Nathan's arm. "Let's boogie."

Nathan was looking at Lisa, sprinting for her cycle. Instantly he knew what he was going to do. He reached into his pocket, grabbed his keys and pressed them into Skeet's hand. "Take my car."

"But—"

"Just park it on the street in front of your house. Put the keys under the floor mat."

"How will you—"

"Do it!" Nathan took off running, catching up to Lisa's cycle just as she was revving the engine. He threw his leg over the seat behind her.

"Get off!"

"No way."

She hesitated. "You'll slow me down. We'll end up in jail."

"I'm riding with you."

"Off, Malone."

"You'd better move it."

"You don't have a helmet."

"Then you'll just have to drive real careful."

The field was almost empty of cars now, and the red cast of the firetruck's lights could be seen swirling in the gloom, hurtling across the field toward the bonfire that glowed and crackled against the dark ground and pale, thickening fog.

"Hang on," Lisa ordered. Leaning forward, she aimed the big Harley in the opposite direction from the fast-approaching truck. In seconds, Nathan was flying through the night, his arms holding her to him.

6

Nathan hunkered down, hanging tight. Riding the Harley was like riding a wild horse, the ground so bumpy that he thought his teeth would jar loose. The dark night surrounded them, and all Nathan saw were blurs of branches shooting past as Lisa kept close to a tree line parallel to a fence. Eventually she hit a dirt road, pelting them with gravel as she turned onto it. The cycle finally hit the solid asphalt of the highway and the ride smoothed.

Nathan watched the white line of the road streak below his feet. His head filled with the noise of the machine and the aroma of her leather jacket. He was freezing, but also wild with the pleasure of the ride and the nearness of Lisa. He would have ridden to the ends of the earth with her, certain that he'd never experienced a greater high than this moment in time.

Lights began to fly past and he realized that they were back in civilization. The cycle slowed, turned again and stopped under glaring lights in a gas station. They both sat on the machine and breathed hard. Slowly the sound of a country song from a nearby car broke into Nathan's consciousness, bringing him back to earth.

"You can let go now," Lisa said.

Unable to feel his cold-numbed fingers, he did so stiffly. He got off the bike, flexed. "We made it." He grinned.

She dismounted the cycle, brushed past him. "I need gas."

He took the pump handle from her, reached into his pocket and pulled out money. "How much?"

"I can buy my own gas."

"I owe you. I invited myself along."

She took a ten-dollar bill from him and headed for the building. Nathan filled the Harley's tank, staring at the beautifully airbrushed red heart emblazoned with her name in fancy letters on a purple ribbon. He'd never felt more alive. Being close to Lisa had awakened him, and he tried to think of a way to keep the feeling going. He glanced around, caught sight of a huge bookstore directly across the street—the kind that stayed open extra late.

She returned, handed him his change just as the pump clicked off. "Can you call your friend to come get you?"

He felt a moment of panic. "Can't I bum a ride

home? I don't live too far from Crestwater. Don't you have to head that way to get home yourself?"

"Afraid I'll dump you out here, Malone?"

"Terrified," he answered truthfully, but kept his tone unemotional. "How about some coffee? I'm cold, aren't you?" He gestured across the street and watched emotions he couldn't read cross her face.

"I need to be going. . . ."

"Come on. It's warm in there. A cup of coffee. What can it hurt?"

Inside the bookstore, which smelled of newly printed books and fresh lemon oil, he bought them each a mug of mocha coffee, then found two easy chairs among the stacks. He watched Lisa sip from her cup and fumbled for a thread of conversation. "You did a brave thing back at the party, standing up to Roddy."

"You're the one who almost got his head knocked off."

"Thanks for intervening. He would have killed me and Skeet and never thought twice about it."

She smiled over the top of her cup, and it was as if someone had turned on a current through his body. "Rod's a bully. He's big, dumb and drunk. In the morning all he'll be is sober."

Nathan grinned. "But still big and dumb?"

"Count on it." She warmed her hands around the cup. "Why did he go after Skeet?"

Nathan shrugged. "I guess because he can. I heard you stood him up last year for the prom. Why?"

She arched an eyebrow. "Because I could." He laughed and she added, "Football season will be over soon and Rod will fade into the background. He won't have staying power, believe me."

Nathan wanted to take her hands in his, but he hesitated. What if she wouldn't stand for it? He asked, "So what kind of music do you like?" She named a couple of bands. "I'm into country," he said. "Not the twangy kind, but the modern kind."

"You mean those songs about somebody doing somebody wrong?"

"I think of them as songs from the heart about life. Skeet and I play in my garage and work up some juice. He's on keyboard. I play guitar. I—um—I've written a few songs myself. Don't expect them to go platinum or anything." She looked more interested. Of course. She liked to write too.

"Ever get any bookings?"

"Not since Morgan Frey's ninth birthday party. Skeet and I were fourteen and the girls thought we were stars." He grinned at the memory. "Our band lacks depth. We need more members."

"A singer?"

"The *right* singer would be good. You a singer?" He didn't dare to hope.

"I can't sing a note."

"So that's a look at my life. How about you? What do you like to write?"

"Nothing that will ever get published."

"You don't know that."

"Sure I do." She took another sip of coffee. "I'll never send them anyplace. The only person who reads my stuff is Fuller, and that's for a grade."

"I want my songs to get published. It would be a kick to hear them on the radio someday."

She continued to drink the coffee, and silence lengthened between them. He searched for something else to say to her, to make her look at him with interest, to have her think he was cool. He should face it: He was dull and boring with a small, uninteresting life. Why should she talk to him?

"What was it like to be homeschooled?" she asked. "Didn't you get lonely?"

"I was alone, but not too lonely. We did things with other homeschoolers—field trips, joint projects. I made it into the citywide spelling bee in seventh grade, but lost in the third round: *excavate* tripped me up. I'm going to use that word in a song someday, just to prove I can. Plus homeschooling has some real perks—the cafeteria lines are really short and the food's incredible."

That made her smile. "Your mother didn't mind having you home all day?"

"She likes to teach. How about you? Have you always gone to Crestwater?" He knew the answer, but he wanted to hear her voice, have her eyes meet his.

"We moved here last January from Valdosta after construction work dried up for Charlie. He got a job here real easy, and there's a lot of building going on in Atlanta. Mom works as an office coordinator for the same construction firm. As for me, well, one high school is pretty much like any other."

"Who's Charlie?"

"The man who lives with Mom and me."

"Your stepdad?"

"No," she said, leaving him to wonder.

His parents were boringly conventional and had been married forever. "Is he the guy who sometimes rides your cycle and picks you up at school?"

"We share my cycle when his truck's down. But the Harley's mine. Charlie bought it for me."

Nathan had many questions he wanted to ask, but she was finished with her coffee, and he saw that she was getting restless. "Want another cup?"

"No thanks." She asked a salesperson passing by for the time.

It was after midnight and his stomach knotted. He didn't want to be late getting home, but he didn't want the evening with Lisa to end. "You going to miss your curfew?" he asked.

She stood. "I don't have curfews. But I'll bet you do, don't you, Malone?"

He felt embarrassed, hating to confess that he still had rules and limits set by his conventional parents. "Until twelve-thirty, but I don't care if I'm late."

"Come on," she said. "I'll drive fast."

Getting on the cycle, he said, "My car's at Skeet's. He's just down the street from me. It'll be best if I park my car in my driveway tonight."

"Whatever," she said, and the engine roared to life.

There was little traffic and she got him to his car in less than twenty minutes. She cut the engine before hitting the top of his street and coasted. At Skeet's street, he hopped in his car, fished out the key from under the floor mat.

"I'll walk this to the corner before I start up." Lisa began pushing the Harley.

"How about a movie next Saturday night?" he whispered loudly, leaning out the window.

"I told you, Malone, I don't date."

Disappointed, he watched her disappear around the corner.

Nathan drove his car into his driveway, jogged to the front door and turned his key in the lock as the hall clock struck the half hour. He had made it. He took the stairs two at a time, quietly slipped into his bedroom and threw himself across his bed, euphoric. He'd spent part of an evening with Lisa and it had left him soaring, and hungry for more of her. He'd get her to go out with him again. He didn't know how, but he would.

He heard one of the twins begin to cry, and soon after, the other started. They would be hungry, and his mother would come down the hall to their room to nurse them. And knowing his mother, she'd peek into his room to check on him. Nathan quickly struggled under the covers, pulling the sheet up just as he heard his door creak open. *All tucked in, Mom.* He heard the door close, and after a few minutes the twins quieted down. Nathan got out of bed, turned on a flashlight and found a legal pad. His head and heart were full of music and he wanted to write it down. Lisa had done that. She'd filled him with hope and fire.

Lisa sat for a long time at the corner, balancing her cycle and looking back at Nathan's house. She saw a dim light go on in an upstairs room and wondered if it was his room. She fumbled in her jacket pockets, searching for a cigarette. She remembered stashing one, but now she couldn't find it. She didn't smoke much, but once in a while she craved a hit of nicotine.

Her search turned up empty and she swore under her breath. Charlie had most likely confiscated it. "You shouldn't smoke," he told her whenever he caught her with a cigarette.

"Why not? It's not as if I'll die of lung cancer."

"It doesn't look ladylike. It's a stinking habit."

"You should talk. Who do you think I steal them from?"

"Just 'cause I smoke don't mean you should."

"You worry too much, Charlie."

Lisa shivered. The light in the window blinked off. She should never have had coffee, or sat and talked to Nathan, or allowed him to put his arms around her waist and press his body against her back. Stupid of her.

She turned on the cycle's engine and the noise splintered the quiet night. Dogs barked. Lisa roared off, determined to put this night behind her—as well as the guileless, blue-eyed boy who wrote country music and made her feel so totally alive.

7

"How was the game?" Karen Malone asked the next morning at breakfast.

"We lost." Nathan sat hunched over his cereal bowl, desperately wishing he was upstairs in bed instead of getting ready to go outside for a morning of yard work with his father, who was already waiting for him in the garage.

"I saw that much in today's paper. I'm asking if you had a good time."

"Mom, it was a football game. I sat in the stands with Skeet. We cheered. We lost. We came home."

"Really?" Her eyes narrowed. "Then why do the clothes you stuffed in the laundry hamper smell like stale beer?"

Nathan went hot all over. "You smelled my clothes?"

"And the inside of your car smells like beer too."

"Aw, come on—"

"*You* come on." She stood at the counter looking furious. "Did you drink last night? Tell me the truth."

"No, I didn't drink. And thanks for the vote of confidence."

"Did Skeet?"

Nathan slammed his spoon down on the table. "We weren't drinking. If you have to know, the beer got spilled on us."

"I don't want you hanging around with kids who drink."

Nathan knew she was on a roll and he didn't want to hear it. He stood up, headed for the garage. "I need to get started. Skeet's coming over later. Grill him if you don't believe me."

"Don't walk away from me while we're talking."

"*You're* talking. I'm not supposed to speak, right? I told you we weren't drinking. I made curfew. And I'll wash my own laundry so the smell of beer won't touch anything sacred." He slammed out of the kitchen.

His father looked up from shaking a bag of grass seed into the dispenser for overseeding the lawn, something he did every fall. "Storm over?"

"It's never over with her. She doesn't trust me."

"She's scared, that's all." Craig paused. "*Were* you drinking last night?"

Nathan threw up his hands. "I can't believe you asked me that! No, I wasn't drinking." He saw no reason to confess that he would have if Roddy hadn't shown up.

"All right. Cool down. I believe you."

Nathan shoved his feet into old gardening sneakers. He stomped over to the push aerator, a piece of equipment with a large heavy drum and spikes for making holes in the lawn. It would leave the hard Georgia clay more pliable and ready to accept the new grass seed his father would scatter. The job was long and difficult, but suddenly Nathan felt like taking his frustration out on the earth. "What's she going to do when I move away next fall? Follow me to college?"

"Don't burn your bridges, son. You may have to take a HOPE Scholarship."

"What! And live at home?" The HOPE Scholarship was money from the state lottery given to students with a B average, and it paid for tuition as long as the student maintained good grades. However, it was only available for students to attend state schools, which would mean Nathan couldn't go away to college, but would have to remain in state, and most likely at home.

"Business is down. We may not be able to afford to send you away."

"That's just great. You know college is my only hope of getting away from her."

"Don't talk as if your mother's trying to ruin your life. College is a privilege, not a right."

"She won't let go, Dad. You know that's true. I

thought the twins would mellow her out. I thought going to Crestwater would get her to step back, but no, she's still dogging me." He kept thinking of Lisa and the extraordinary freedom she had to come and go, to not have a curfew.

"Your mother's been through a lot. This whole family's been through a lot."

"Old news," Nathan said stubbornly. "No one can change the past and I shouldn't be the one to pay because Mom's afraid."

"They're my fears too," his father said quietly, but quickly added, "Listen, she *will* get involved with the twins, especially as they get older. She's tapped out right now, tired all the time. Cut her some slack, okay?"

"Why do I have to be the one?"

"Because you're the one who matters most." His father looked resigned. "And because I've given my whole life to make things better for her. To make it up to her somehow."

Nathan felt deflated. No matter how their history got discussed, it always came back to ground zero. He used to think that their family history was a vicious circle, but now that he was older he saw that it was more like a spiral, moving not round and round, but downward, ever downward.

Nathan was in his room picking on his guitar that afternoon when Skeet came by after finishing his shift at the grocery store. "Hey, man. I'm busting to know what happened last night." Skeet tossed his wadded apron onto the bed and plopped on the floor in front of Nathan. "I know you rode off with Lisa. Where'd you go?"

"As far away from the field as we could get." Nathan perked up. Talking about Lisa was a sure way to bring him out of his funk.

"Which would be . . . ?"

Nathan grinned. "We ended up having coffee at some bookstore and talking. Then she brought me home."

"Oh man, you lucky dog!"

"It was a wild ride. I don't think the girl knows the meaning of fear."

"And you got to hold her body? You actually put your arms around her?"

"I got to hang on to her for my *life*. You ever ride across a bumpy field on a Harley?"

"Not lately." Skeet pulled a candy bar from his shirt pocket and offered half to Nathan, who refused it. "So now what?"

"That's what I'm trying to figure out." He put down the guitar. "The girl's got secrets, Skeet."

"How do you know this? Did she say, 'I've got a secret'?"

Nathan shook his head. "She didn't have to. I just know it in my gut."

"And you want to know her secrets."

"I do."

"Gee, most guys just want to get in her pants."

Nathan scowled. "That's crude."

"And that thought's never crossed your mind?"

"Knock it off, Skeet. Don't talk about her like she's some kind of sex prize."

Skeet looked contrite. "Sorry, man. I just can't believe you're immune to that part. She's beautiful, and every guy at school wants her. What makes you think you can score? And I don't mean in a crude way. But score with her in a real way."

"Maybe I can't. But I won't know if I don't try."

"Got a game plan?"

Nathan sat back down, picked up his guitar. "Maybe I'll write a song for her."

"Need my input?" Skeet wiggled his fingers.

"Not yet. I'll let you know." Nathan couldn't concentrate with Skeet staring up at him, so after a few minutes he set down the instrument. "Want to shoot some hoops?"

"Great!"

They passed through the kitchen, where Nathan's mother was busy creating supper. "Hey, Skeet."

"What's cooking, Mrs. M?"

"Meatloaf, mashed potatoes and gravy."

Nathan remained sullen. She knew he loved her special meatloaf, and this was her way of saying she was sorry about their fight that morning.

"There's plenty," Karen said. "Want to stay?"

Skeet's face broke into an eager smile. "You bet! Double my gravy portion."

Nathan led the way out the door to the side of the house where the basketball hoop hung, not yet willing to accept her peace offering.

If Nathan thought he'd be able to have any kind of familiarity with Lisa on Monday, he was wrong. She didn't come to school for two days, and when she did show up, she acted preoccupied and rushed out of Fuller's class like a whirlwind. Nathan hardly had a chance to speak to her.

Fuller pulled a pop quiz on Thursday and passed back the results on Friday. Nathan had scored a ninety on the test, but attached to it was his first creative paper as 705, and it was a spiderweb of red ink. His stomach knotted as he read the teacher's notes. Fuller had found the paper "pedantic, plodding and a rehash of old ideas." He'd urged Nathan to try something "fresh and innovative" for his next effort. The teacher had added, "You write well-constructed sentences, so I know you have a command of grammar rules. But good writing isn't always about rules. It's also about feelings and emotions offered in an original format. Think outside the box."

For some reason, Fuller's criticism stung him like the tentacles of a jellyfish. Instead of impressing the teacher, he'd humiliated himself. He wondered what Fuller had written on Lisa's paper, then remembered that she'd skipped that day. And how about 454? What wonderful praise had Fuller heaped on that person's paper?

"You up for a session?" Skeet's voice broke into Nathan's dark thoughts. "I don't have to work this afternoon, and I don't want to hang around my house."

"Sure." Nathan shoved his papers into his notebook and headed for the parking lot with Skeet.

"Bad news?"

"No. Just a test." By habit, Nathan searched the lot the instant they were outside.

"She already left," Skeet said. "I saw her take off a few minutes ago."

Nathan shrugged. "It doesn't matter."

"You giving up?"

"Do I look like a quitter?"

Skeet grinned. "You're the man."

Later, Nathan raised the garage door, plugged in his electric guitar, and let Skeet cut loose on the keyboard. Nathan preferred his acoustical guitar, but at the moment he felt like making noise, and his mother and the twins were off shopping, so no one was there to shush him. He let the music crank and, pulling fevered, frenzied sounds from the steel strings, closed his eyes and let the music take him to another zone. He was aware of nothing until Skeet's playing fell off and he opened his eyes to complain and then saw why Skeet had stopped.

At the end of his driveway, Lisa sat wrapped in

leather and staring at him from the seat of her Harley. His heart leaped. He laid down the guitar and started for the door. She quickly backed her Harley onto the street, kicked off.

"Lisa!" he yelled. "Wait! Lisa!"

By the time he'd sprinted to the end of his driveway, she was gone.

8

Nathan squirmed through the remainder of the weekend, arrived early at school on Monday and waited in the parking lot for Lisa, hoping that today wouldn't be one of the days that Charlie's truck was broken. He was rewarded by the sound and sight of her cycle just after the first tardy bell. He didn't care if he was late to first period, he was going to talk to her. She pulled into her space and he stepped from behind the car parked next to it. "Good morning."

She looked startled. "Same to you." She unstrapped her book bag from the seat. He eased in front of her. "Are you stalking me, Malone?"

"Why did you come by my house on Saturday?"

"I was out for a ride. You own the streets?"

"Why my street?"

She tried to shove past him, but she couldn't. "Don't let it go to your head, Malone. You don't mean anything to me."

He jammed his hands into the pockets of his jacket. "Sure I do, Lisa. You just haven't accepted it yet." He had no idea where he'd gotten the nerve to say such a thing. Chalk it up to being angry.

She rolled her eyes. "Guys are so vain. A cup of coffee and a ride home is not the basis for a lasting relationship. Now excuse me."

"If you would like to really hear us play, Skeet and I are holding an audition Saturday afternoon in my garage for a drummer—some guy Skeet met at work who thinks he'd like a stab at it."

"I hope it goes well for you." She'd walked around to the opposite side.

"Three o'clock," he added as the last bell sounded and she hurried toward the building.

Lisa was cool to him in Fuller's class. Nathan didn't push it. He held out hope that his invitation wouldn't be ignored. Whether she admitted it or not, there was an undercurrent flowing between them. Like static electricity that snapped at unexpected moments, he could feel it. And he craved it.

On Friday, Fuller collected more of the class's original papers. When the bell rang Nathan was surprised when Lisa turned in her desk and asked, "Did you submit one of your songs to Fuller?"

"No."

"Why not?"

"They're private."

She looked skeptical. "You want some big country singer to sing your songs, but you don't want someone as good as Fuller to judge them first, is that it? You can't have it both ways, Malone."

"They're not the kind of poetry Fuller would appreciate. Songs need music to make them sound right. You ever read the words to a song, a song you might love when it's played? It can sound pretty dumb because the words depend on the music to drive them."

"Coward," she said, then picked up her books and left.

He cleaned the garage on Saturday, rolled out the piece of carpet he and Skeet used for practice, even vacuumed it, and set up a side table with sodas on ice. Skeet was impressed. "All for an audition with a drummer? He may suck."

"We should at least look like we're serious and sort of professional. Okay—semiprofessional," he amended when Skeet gave him a kooky look.

"What's next? A tour bus?"

The drummer arrived right on time, a kid named Larry who proceeded to set up his gear and tell Nathan and Skeet how his former band had played a few bar mitzvah parties, some birthday celebrations for socially connected Atlanta debutantes, and a country club before breaking up.

"We're not into rock," Nathan explained.

"I can dig it," Larry said.

Except that he couldn't. The rhythm of country seemed to totally defeat Larry, and after half an hour, Nathan was ready to throw his drum set out the door. He was edgy too because he kept hoping Lisa would show, and just as he was giving up on the possibility, she rolled into his driveway. His heart leaped and he couldn't hide a smile.

Lisa wasn't alone. Her rider was the girl Nathan had seen her with at the football game. Lisa boldly walked into the garage, and the girl followed hesitantly. "Are these auditions open?" Lisa asked.

"To you they are, baby," Larry called out.

She gave him a look that would have peeled paint and turned toward Nathan. "This is my friend, Jodie Price. She's a hell of a singer and you should give her a chance."

Skeet walked over. "We don't need a singer."

Jodie pulled on Lisa's arm. "Let's go. I told you this was a bad idea."

Nathan saw the scared look on Jodie's face and realized that Lisa had strong-armed her into coming. He also felt instantly sorry for the girl because he knew what it was to be an outsider. "Did Lisa tell you we're country?"

"My favorite," Jodie said. She was a short girl with a round face, short dark hair and brown eyes. She was heavy, but pretty in her way. She kept fidgeting, and Nathan figured Jodie would rather be anyplace but here.

"We should give her a try," Nathan told Skeet.

Skeet grimaced, but returned to his keyboard.

"How about some classic Patsy Cline?" Nathan picked up his acoustical guitar. It felt funny to be auditioning people for their band, more their hobby than anything else.

"I know 'Crazy' and 'Sweet Dreams,' " Jodie said. "Actually, I know all her songs."

"Let's try 'Crazy.' " Nathan looked straight at Lisa.

She ignored his look, walked over to the table, plucked a soda from the cooler and sat on an old folding chair.

Nathan played a few riffs. Skeet picked up the melody, and even Larry managed to come in softly with his snare drum. Jodie stepped up, opened her mouth and sang the words with a magical timbre that sent goose bumps up Nathan's back. Who knew that such a voice could come out of this shy, plump little girl? *Lisa had known.*

They stopped and started a few times, but eventually got through the song. When the last note had faded, Lisa jumped up, clapping. "Didn't I tell you she was good?"

"You're good," Nathan told Jodie, who turned red and shuffled her feet.

Skeet came over. "Yes. But we never planned on adding a singer."

"It's all right," Jodie said, dropping her gaze to the floor.

"You should practice some more together," Lisa interjected. "See what comes of it. What kind of a band are you if you don't have a singer?"

"Want to try it again next week?" Nathan asked.

Jodie shrugged. "I—I guess so."

"Give Skeet a way to get hold of you."

"What about me?" Larry asked.

"Same thing." He turned to Lisa. "Take a walk with me."

"Where?"

"Around back."

He unlatched the high wooden gate and led her down the path to his mother's eye-popping backyard of winding trails, clusters of trees, shrubs, and flowers, and gurgling koi pond. Many of the leaves were tinged with the colors of autumn. By November, the trees would be dormant and bare.

"Whoa," Lisa said when they rounded the corner of the house. "Some backyard, Malone."

"My mother's hobby." He kept his eyes on Lisa. "Why did you bring Jodie over here?"

"To sing with your band."

"Skeet and I just mess around. We don't have a serious band."

"You should. You sounded pretty good to me."

"Jodie would never have done this if you hadn't dragged her."

"So? She's got a great voice. She just needs confidence. Your band can give that to her, and in the bargain, your band will be better. I'm doing you both a favor."

"Where do you know her from?" He never saw Lisa hang with anyone at school, and Jodie was the type who faded into the woodwork in a school the size of Crestwater.

"She lives in my apartment building. I heard her singing out on the playground one day last summer. She didn't see me. She was sitting on a swing. The place was empty and she was just singing out loud. I told her I thought she sounded great. She was embarrassed, but once we got to know each other, we became friends. She has talent, and your band's a good start for her. Not everyone can be on *Star Search* or *American Idol.*"

"What do you get out of it, Lisa?" He kept digging for Lisa's motives, which he figured were present, but he couldn't grasp what they were. "What exactly do you want?"

She didn't say anything at first. He kept looking at her, at her violet eyes, at her lips, full and shimmering with gloss. It made his knees weak. "No one can give me what I want, Malone." She surprised him by looping her arm through his. "Show me around. Where I live we only get flowers planted at the entrance. The place is mostly asphalt, parked cars and a few scraggly trees, watered daily by dogs. I'm telling you, those trees are toxic. No one can go near them."

Nathan walked with Lisa. He knew the gardens well, since he helped his mother tend them, so he talked about specific plants and apologized for what wasn't blooming. "You should really come in the spring," he said. "I'll bet there are a thousand flowers then."

She seemed totally into the tour and for once he was glad his mother had taken such pains with the yard.

They stopped at the koi pond and Lisa sat on the bench, leaned out over the water and watched the exotic fish come to the surface in a school of fluttering fins.

"They're beggars," Nathan said. "We can hand-feed them."

"Really? Can I?"

"I'll have to go get some bread from the house."

"No, that's okay. Some other day."

Did that mean she might actually come again? He'd been trying to get her attention and spend more time with her, and all it might have taken was an invitation to feed some fish.

She sat back, closed her eyes and breathed in the air. She was so beautiful that he wanted to kiss her. Of course, she'd probably push him into the pond if he tried. Her eyes opened and focused on the magnificent magnolia tree in the center of the yard. "Big tree."

"Mom planted it when I was three."

Lisa studied the beds around the tree, set off by a meandering row of bricks and Spanish tile. "You know, it sort of looks like there was something else there at one time. Before the flower beds and tree."

"There was."

"Tell me."

His heart pounded and his mouth tasted bone-dry. It was the thing his family never spoke about. "We used to have a swimming pool. Mom liked the tiles too much to rip them out."

"And your parents covered it over? We have a pool

at my complex, but it's toxic too." She wrinkled her nose. "Too many little kids peeing in it. So why did you all fill yours in with dirt? Too much trouble to take care of? Your mom wanted gardens and trees instead?"

The pounding in Nathan's ears was almost a roar. He wanted to tell her but wasn't sure if he should. It was their family business, and besides, it might turn her off, one thing he didn't want to do. Nathan took a deep breath and stared out across the sun-splashed lawn. "We covered it over because it's where my sister drowned."

9

"She *drowned*?"

"When she was six. It was a long time ago." Nathan felt hot and knew color was seeping up his neck. He should have kept his mouth shut.

Lisa stared at him, a range of emotions he couldn't decipher playing across her pretty face. He knew she had questions, but he hoped with everything inside of him that she wouldn't ask any. He'd said too much already. "That's very sad," she finally said, and reached over and stroked his hand.

He jerked back, but only because it was so unexpected. "We don't talk about it," he said, regretting pulling away from her.

She didn't seem to be bothered by his rejection. The koi thrashed at the pond's surface, and Nathan watched Lisa's reflection undulate in the water. He saw something on her face that he couldn't describe but that spoke to his heart. *Sadness? Understanding?* More than anything, he wanted to put his arms around her, hold her close. He could have spent forever next to her, imagining her in his arms with this mysterious thread somehow connecting them.

"Forever" ended abruptly when Skeet crashed through the foliage. "There you guys are! Jodie thought you'd run off and left her." His pique turned to apology when he looked at their faces. "Sorry, dude."

Lisa jumped up. "I've got to get home too."

The three of them hurried back to the garage, and Jodie looked relieved when she saw them. Larry was long gone. Dusk had fallen and the driveway was dark. Nathan turned on a light and watched the girls climb onto the Harley. "You sing great, Jodie," he called out. "Next week again, you hear?"

"I'll be here," Jodie said.

"You can come too," he said to Lisa.

"I'll bring Jodie, but I can't stay." Lisa was back to her cool, elusive self.

A wind had kicked up and Nathan watched them drive off, feeling as cold and scattered as the dry leaves tumbling around his feet.

Lisa eased into the dark apartment. "Mom?" No answer. Then she remembered it was bingo night at the Catholic church. Her mother wasn't Catholic, but she loved bingo.

"Lisa? Back here," Charlie called.

She flipped on a lamp, tossed her book bag on the sofa and went down the hall to the apartment's third bedroom, where Charlie had set up the television, DVD, his recliner and an over-the-hill couch. He muted the TV with the remote control and waved her over. He was freshly showered, his long hair pulled back in a ponytail. He smelled of leather and lime soap. "I made some soup for us," he said. "It's on the stove. You hungry?"

"Jodie and I stopped for a burger."

"How'd her audition go?"

"She wowed them."

Charlie grinned. "So you were right about them needing her, weren't you?"

Lisa tugged off her boots, propped her feet on the old scarred coffee table. "They asked her back next week."

"They any good?"

"They've got a ways to go before they can play in public."

"And the young man?"

"What about him?" She kept seeing Nathan's face, almost expressionless, when he told her about his drowned sister. Lisa was intensely curious about it, but knew how it felt to have someone pile on questions you didn't want to answer. Some secrets were best left buried.

"You still like him?"

"I don't like anybody, Charlie. Not in the way you're thinking. You know I can't."

71

"That's all in your head, little girl. You told me you wanted to try out everything, remember? Well, loving somebody is part of the trying-out business."

"Not for me." She stared at the figures on TV, characters running around wildly in some movie, looking extremely stupid without a sound track. "Why do you stay, Charlie? Mom's never here. I'm—well, you know how I am. Why do you waste your time on us?"

"Your mom's not a strong person, Lisa," Charlie drawled after a minute of reflection. "Not all her fault," he added. "Life's just worn her down. You and me *are* strong. So we pick up the slack, make it easier for those who aren't strong. This young man—"

"Nathan Malone," she said, hating to say his name because a name made a person real. It breathed life into someone who otherwise remained in the shadows.

"This Nathan, is he strong?"

She thought about that, about the way he'd looked at her when she told him to get off her bike that night in the woods, about how he'd cornered her in the parking lot and forced her to listen to him, about the look on his face when he'd told her about his sister. "He doesn't discourage easily. Yes, he's strong."

Charlie leaned back in his recliner. "That's good, Lisa. 'Cause you're going to need a strong one."

The Saturday jam sessions proved to be the highlight of Nathan's weeks. Not only was their band improving, their sound maturing, but it was also when he could see Lisa without the clutter of the classroom surrounding them. She had proven standoffish, and he'd been unable to connect with her as he had that night in the bookstore or the afternoon by the koi pond. Every day she rushed out of Fuller's class, offering Nathan a breezy goodbye, acting as if they'd never shared a moment together. On Saturdays, she brought Jodie to Nathan's garage and either waited for her to finish or left and returned for her later. By November, when the first cold snap hit Atlanta, Nathan was desperate to be alone with her again.

"Keep Jodie and Larry busy," Nathan instructed Skeet one Saturday before the others arrived.

"How?"

"Figure it out. I want to get Lisa off to myself for a little while."

"You've been making cow eyes at her for a month and she hasn't taken the hint," Skeet said. "What makes you think a few minutes alone with her today will make a difference?"

"If I wanted an argument, I'd have asked my mother," Nathan growled. "She's out with the twins. Dad's playing golf. I want a chance to be alone with Lisa. Are you going to help me or not?"

Skeet bowed from the waist. "I'm your servant."

The practice went well, and as soon as it was over, Skeet stepped up to Jodie. "Hey, can you and Larry take a sec to go over some parts of the last number with me?"

"What about Nathan?" Jodie asked.

"Don't need him for this."

Nathan set his guitar aside. "Mom left a plateful of cookies for us in the kitchen."

Larry whooped. "I *love* your mother's cookies!"

"It's cold out here," Lisa said. She'd been sitting in an old lawn chair, flipping through a magazine.

"I'll brew some hot chocolate," Nathan said.

"That would be good," Jodie said eagerly.

Nathan turned to Lisa. "Could you help me carry stuff?"

She hesitated, but Jodie gave her a pleading look. "All right," she said, not sounding happy about it. She followed Nathan indoors.

The kitchen looked spotless, and the smell of chocolate chip cookies spiced the air. Nathan pulled a gallon of milk from the refrigerator and poured some into a pan, rummaged in the pantry for cocoa and sugar, all the while maintaining a stream of conversation. "You were right about Jodie. She's great. Larry's talking about getting us a gig or two for the holidays. He has connections from his old days and we think we might give it a try—"

"Nathan, it's okay. You don't have to talk me to death. I don't mind helping you with the food. I don't mind being alone with you."

He was glad for the dim light. She couldn't see how embarrassed her words made him feel. He put the pan of milk on the stove and turned on the gas burner.

"Okay, you found me out. I do want to be alone with you."

"Why?"

"Because you never even look my way at school."

She crossed her arms. "It's nothing personal."

He forced a laugh. "Well, it feels personal. It feels like you think there's something wrong with me. Like I'm not worth another conversation, or another cup of coffee. Why can't you stand being alone with me?"

"That isn't true."

"Then why can't we be friends?"

"We are. I found your band a singer, didn't I?"

"You did that for Jodie. The fact that she helps our band is bonus points. Not all of us are projects for Lisa to manage, you know. What do you get out of it?"

"I—it's complicated. My life is complicated."

"How so? Have you got a job?" She shook her head. "Then what? You don't have curfews. You cut school at will. You don't hang with anyone. What's complicated?"

"Why do you care?"

"Because *you* care. You stand up for me and Skeet to a guy like Roddy. You become an advocate for a girl like Jodie. Your 'I don't give a damn' routine doesn't hold up with me."

"I'll work on it." She looked shaken, tried to brush past him.

He caught her arm. "Not so fast." And before he could stop himself, he'd pulled her against his chest and kissed her full and hard on the mouth. She fought him at first, but he didn't let go, and as the kiss lengthened, it deepened. His blood sang in his head, tore through his veins like wildfire. He raised his hands and cupped her face, pushed his tongue between her lips. She didn't resist, but put her arms around him and kissed him willingly.

The hiss of milk boiling over on the stove was what finally seeped through Nathan's consciousness and broke them apart. They stood staring at each other while the milk sizzled and a burning smell singed the air. Nathan's hands were shaking and his heart was almost jumping from his chest. Lisa's eyes looked huge and deep. Her breath was ragged and louder than the boiling milk. She stepped backward, turned to the stove and shut off the flame. "It's a mess," she mumbled, and he was certain that she wasn't talking only about the burned milk.

He came up behind her, wanting to touch her, hold her, but she sidestepped him. "Don't," she said.

Nathan walked across the floor to the kitchen island. He rested his palms on the cool granite, licked his lips, and tasted her all over again. "I'm not sorry," he said.

"Nothing's changed," she said, sounding stubborn.

Her words wounded him. He'd put himself on the line with that kiss, opened his heart and invited her inside, and now she was pulling back. Again. "Sure it has." He crossed to the refrigerator. "We have to heat more milk."

*   *   *

There were only three days of school the following week because of Thanksgiving. Lisa missed the first two and on the third slipped into her seat in Fuller's class just as the bell rang. Nathan ached with frustration. Had she not come to school simply to avoid him? He'd thought about calling her but kept losing his nerve. Plus, there was no listing for her in the phone book. Better to deal with her face to face. But at the moment, he was staring at her back and Fuller was talking about poets Nathan had no interest in. Lisa lifted her hair and gathered it into a barrette, and Nathan was left to stare at the nape of her beautiful neck. He wanted to put his hands around her neck and shout, *Don't you know you're making me crazy!*

". . . poets today have difficulty being heard because poetry has few advocates in today's world," Fuller was saying.

Nathan squinted at the base of Lisa's neck, where a tiny grid of blue dots disappeared into her hairline. Had she started a tattoo and then changed her mind? He'd always wanted one, but never had the courage to get one. His mother would have hit the roof and grounded him for life if he had. But Lisa—well, she apparently could do whatever she wanted.

". . . read a nice piece of work to you today." Fuller's voice broke through Nathan's thoughts. "It's a love poem by one of our own and resonates without being cloying. I thought it quite good. It was written by student seven-oh-five."

Nathan's heart seized.

10

Nathan heard shoes shuffle, papers rustle. Usually Fuller called out every number except Nathan's, and he read student 454's work more often than any other. Nathan slumped low in his desk chair, cut his eyes sideways, wondered if he was wearing a sign announcing, LOOK HERE! I'M STUDENT 705! He sure hoped not. He'd tried for weeks to write well enough to be picked, but his work always came back swimming in red ink. According to Fuller, it lacked originality. It lacked conviction. He scribbled, "You write well, but it feels forced and dry"—whatever *that* meant. And now today, while Nathan was in total turmoil because of Lisa, Fuller had discovered something worthy to be read aloud. His stomach tightened.

Fuller cleared his throat and began reading Nathan's work.

"I stand and watch you from afar.
I wish upon you, like a star.
You see me not.
You come.
You go.
Still, I love you better than you know."

Fuller lowered the paper and a girl on the side of the room said, "That's just *so* romantic."

"Why?" Fuller asked.

Nathan's ears felt on fire. He slunk lower in his seat. He'd written the poem late one night when he'd been longing for Lisa. The words had come quickly, easily, like water from a faucet. He'd been nuts to turn it in as an assignment.

No one spoke, and Fuller said, "It's short and to the point. And we like it because it came from the writer's heart, not his head. And that, my future Writers of America, is where all good writing comes from—a person's heart. And once you tap into it, your work will come alive. Trust me."

Nathan left the room slowly that day, not wanting to talk to anyone, especially Lisa, because he was certain he was wearing the poem's authorship across his face like a billboard. He was suddenly glad about the long holiday weekend. He and Skeet hadn't scheduled practice either. It meant four days without seeing Lisa. Four days. Ninety-six hours. Five thousand, seven hundred and sixty minutes to distance himself from the confession of his heart, now made public.

* * *

On Friday afternoon Skeet came over and asked, "Can I borrow your wheels to go see Jodie?"

Nathan was shooting baskets in the driveway. "Why?"

"I want to see her."

Nathan stopped mid-dribble, tucked the ball under his arm and stared hard at his friend. "You got something going with Jodie?"

Skeet's face turned beet red. "We—um—have been talking on our cells and seeing each other at school."

"Why didn't you tell me you liked her?"

Skeet shrugged. "I didn't know how. You've had your head up your butt for weeks. I thought you would notice eventually."

Nathan shook his head, felt apologetic and stupid at the same time. "I should have noticed. Sorry, man."

"So can I take your car?"

"Jodie lives in the same apartment building as Lisa, doesn't she?" Skeet nodded. "Give me fifteen to clean up and I'll drive you over myself." He tossed the ball into the garage.

"I thought you might," Skeet said, with a wry grin.

Magnolia Gardens, the apartment complex where Lisa and Jodie lived, was a maze of yellow and brown rundown-looking buildings with a faded red tennis court, sans nets, and a pool long past its prime. Small signs pointed the way to the back. Jodie lived near a

80

yard full of little kids climbing on old playground equipment. Cars were parked everywhere, and Nathan ended up blocking in a car that Skeet said belonged to Jodie's divorced mother.

Jodie opened her door, and the smile she beamed at Skeet told the story of how she felt about him. Nathan couldn't believe he'd been so blind and preoccupied not to have seen it before. "Lisa lives in the left front ground-floor apartment through the next stairwell over," Jodie told him.

Nathan thanked her and beat a quick retreat. A wreath made of fall foliage and orange ribbon hung on the scarred front door of Lisa's apartment. Nathan wiped his sweating palms on his jeans and rang the bell.

"Can I help you, son?" A man's voice came from behind Nathan.

Nathan walked back out to the parking lot to where the man was working under the raised hood of an old truck. He wore a ponytail and was dressed in dirty jeans, a sweatshirt and a jacket. "I'm Charlie Terry," he said, wiping his hands on a soiled rag.

"Nathan Malone." They shook hands.

"I'm guessing you're looking for Lisa."

"I was in the area. Brought my friend to visit Jodie." The excuse sounded lame even to Nathan's ears.

"Lisa's out with her mom doing some Christmas shopping."

Of course. His mother had taken off early to do the same thing. His father had twins duty.

"They've been gone awhile, so I expect they'll be back soon. If you want to wait around, you can."

Nathan didn't have anything else to do. He couldn't barge in on Skeet and Jodie, and he couldn't drive off and leave Skeet. "If you don't mind."

Charlie smiled. He was tall and well muscled. His skin was deeply tanned and his hands looked like worn leather. His voice, thick as honey, sounded Southern. "You know anything about engines?"

"Just that cars need them to move."

That made Charlie laugh. "This old heap should be sold for scrap, but I keep hobbling her together. Cheaper than a new one." He ducked back under the hood.

Nathan leaned in to see a maze of wires, and the smell of oil assailed him. "What's wrong?"

"I think it's the alternator." When Nathan said nothing, Charlie added, "It sends electrical current to the battery. If the alternator doesn't work, the car won't start."

"I thought the battery had the electricity."

Charlie cocked his head and grinned. "You really *don't* know much about cars."

"Or girls either," Nathan said before thinking.

Charlie laughed, straightened. "Women are a mystery, all right. Even Shakespeare thought so." Then he proceeded to quote several passages about women from different Shakespearean plays. Nathan recognized only a few, but Charlie's rich voice made each line sound heavy with meaning. Charlie finished with, " 'Who ever loved, that loved not at first sight?' That's from *As You Like It*."

Was Charlie making fun of him? Had he figured out how much Nathan cared about Lisa? And how little Lisa cared about him? "There's been a few songs written about it too," Nathan said. "I guess no one can figure them out."

Charlie looked amused. "Not that we don't keep trying." He worked with the wires, attaching several to a black gizmo. "Now, hooking up an alternator, this makes sense. Machines are fixable and they're logical too." Finally he said, "Get in and turn the key. Let's see if I've done this right."

Nathan scooted across the torn bench seat and turned the key. The engine sputtered, then came alive. He hopped out. "That's pretty cool."

"What—making a truck start? A monkey could do it if you showed him how."

"They say a monkey could write a novel if you leave him at it long enough. That doesn't mean the novel will be any *good*."

Charlie slapped Nathan's shoulder. "Right again."

Nathan felt pleased that Charlie seemed to approve of him, because he knew that even though the man wasn't Lisa's father, Lisa thought a great deal of him. Nathan poked his head under the hood of Charlie's truck and was studying the perplexing engine when Lisa's voice asked, "What are you doing here, Malone?"

Nathan jumped and banged his head on the edge of the raised hood. He saw stars.

"Now look what you've done," Charlie said. "He's bleeding."

Nathan reached up. His hair felt sticky, and when he looked at his hand, he saw blood.

"Are you all right?" Lisa looked anxious.

"I—I think so. Do you have a twin sister? I see two of you."

Charlie chuckled. "Take him inside and fix him up, girl."

Once inside the apartment, Lisa sat Nathan on a chair in the small dining area and clamped a folded paper towel onto his head wound. "I'll be right back."

He waited, looking the place over. It was sparsely furnished, with few decorations on the walls. The apartment looked lived in, but not homey. The front door opened and a woman entered carrying several department store sacks. "You okay? Charlie told me what happened. I'm Jill Lindstrom, Lisa's mother." She was an older version of Lisa, except that her hair was bleached blond with dark roots showing.

"I'm all right," he said.

"Let me see." She lifted the paper towel. "Scalp cuts bleed something fierce, but I don't think it's too deep."

Lisa returned with a damp cloth and antiseptic cream. The two women hovered over Nathan, making him feel nervous and embarrassed. A little cut didn't warrant so much attention. After a few minutes they were finished, and Nathan said, "Thanks."

Jill sized him up. "So you go to school with Lisa."

It was more a statement than a question, but Nathan said, "Yes, ma'am. I'm Nathan."

" 'Ma'am?' " She looked amused. "Don't call me ma'am, makes me feel old."

Nathan colored. He'd been raised to say *yes, sir* and *yes, ma'am*. "I—I didn't mean—"

Jill squeezed his arm. "Why, aren't you the cutest thing! You're blushing." She turned to Lisa. "Hang on to him, honey. Gentlemen are hard to come by."

"Mother!"

"Well, he is cute," Jill insisted. "He's adorable. And just look at those eyelashes. Boys shouldn't have eyelashes that long. It's not fair."

Lisa shot her mother a threatening look. "Don't you have something to *do,* Mom?"

Jill smiled brightly. "Reckon I can put away the things we bought." She went over and picked up the sacks. "Now, you come back any time you want, Nathan. Any friend of Lisa's is always welcome here." She breezed down the hall.

Lisa waited until a door shut, then turned to Nathan. "You sure you're all right?"

He saw that she was flustered and he pressed his advantage. "Maybe I should come over tomorrow for a checkup."

"Don't push it, Malone."

He caught her wrist. "Why do you always call me by my last name?"

"First names are too personal."

"I've heard you call others by their first names. Why be personal with them and not me?"

"You ask too many questions."

He eased her onto his lap, felt her tense up. "I'm not going to bite, Lisa."

"Why are you here anyway?"

He explained about Skeet and Jodie. "Did you know they liked each other?"

"Sure. Didn't you?"

"I was clueless." He rested his hand against the small of her back, felt the warmth of her skin through her clothing. "Did you plan for them to hit it off?"

"No one can plan those kinds of things. But I was hoping they'd like each other. And now they do."

"So why them and not us?"

She stiffened and her eyes looked shuttered. "There is no us, Malone."

"There could be." He got an idea, lifted her up and stood. "Tell you what. Come home with me today. My mother's one of those Christmas freaks who has to put up a tree right after Thanksgiving. We'll be decorating it tonight. You can help." She started to shake her head, but he caught her face between his palms and kissed her lightly. "I'm your patient, remember? You need to keep an eye on me, see to it that I don't slip into a coma from this nasty head wound I suffered while trying to help fix Charlie's truck. It's the least you can do, Lisa."

11

"Tell me, Lisa, have you chosen a college yet?" Nathan's mother asked at dinner that night. His parents had been surprised when he had shown up with Lisa and announced that she was staying for dinner and the tree-decorating ritual. He'd never brought a girl home for dinner before, plus they'd always done tree trimming only as a family. Karen had eyed Lisa like an interloper and even flashed Nathan a few questioning looks that he ignored.

"Not yet," Lisa said. "I'm not planning on going to college."

Nathan glanced at his mother, knowing that Lisa had uttered heresy. Her answer had surprised him too, though.

"Nathan's going to college," Karen declared.

"He should," Lisa said. "He's smart."

"Lisa's smart too," Nathan said, feeling a need to defend her.

"So what will you do in lieu of college?" Karen asked. The twins, in matching high chairs beside the table, sucked on matching pacifiers. At four months, neither could sit up on her own, but the chairs had a semi-reclining position, and the two together in matching reindeer outfits looked adorable.

"I stopped making plans years ago."

Nathan wondered what she meant by that.

Just then Abby dropped her pacifier and let out a wail. Lisa bent and retrieved the thing. "I'll go rinse it off."

"I'll do it." Karen took the pacifier.

The moment she left the dining room, Nathan's father said, "It's okay if you don't want to go to college. It's not a capital offense."

"My mother already has the twins enrolled," Nathan added, irritated by his mother's third degree.

Karen swept back into the room. "What about your parents? What do they want you to do?"

"They pretty much let me do what I want."

Karen looked shocked. "Really?"

"It's a long story."

Nathan watched Lisa withdraw. She wasn't going to say anything that revealed more than she wanted. Lisa had walls around her that no one breached. He willed his mother to change the subject.

Karen apparently got his mental message because she said to his father, "Did you get the tree set up?"

He and Nathan had wrestled the overly large fir into its tree stand earlier. "It's standing. But I still need to put the lights on it."

"And I need to get the girls in bed."

Lisa slid her chair away from the table. "How about if Nathan and I clean up?"

"Thank you." Karen's voice was crisp.

Alone in the kitchen with Lisa, Nathan said, "I'd like to hear your long story someday."

Lisa looked over at the refrigerator at Molly's drawing hanging dead center. "And I'd like to hear yours."

Nathan glanced at the artwork. It had hung there for so long, he sometimes failed to see it. "Not much to tell. I was three when it happened. Molly was six. She sneaked out of the house during naptime and drowned in the pool. I don't really remember much about it at all."

"Do you remember Molly?"

He shrugged. "Sometimes I think I do. But I get the images all mixed up with the photos Mom keeps of her in our photo albums. So I can't really say for sure that I remember her. But that's okay, because Mom never lets any of us forget her."

Lisa reached over and removed a glass that Nathan was holding. "You were squeezing it so tight, I thought you might break it," she explained quietly.

"I guess you've seen enough of my blood for one day, huh?"

"After we finish here, can I see your room?" she asked, changing the subject.

Nathan took her all over the house, room by room. She asked questions, and he wondered what she thought of his lifestyle, different from hers. He wondered too what *did* matter to her. She seemed more relaxed than ever, smitten with the twins, and not intimidated by his parents. The girl was a puzzle and a surprise, all in one package.

They ended up in the basement, right outside the door of what had been his classroom for so many years. She asked, "Do you miss being homeschooled?"

"No."

"But you're not crazy about Crestwater either."

"I don't feel like I fit either place. This is too isolated. The other, too fragmented. I'm not sure my mom did me any favors."

"My mother couldn't have done it for me. Charlie could have, but he had to work to pay the bills. Besides, he never graduated from high school."

"You're kidding. He was quoting Shakespeare to me."

Lisa smiled. "I never said he wasn't educated. He reads all the time. He's the smartest man I know. Maybe even smarter than Fuller. He took courses at a college but he says he screwed some things up. I don't know the story, but he likes working with his hands outdoors, and he's been good to us. He understands life can give you a bad hand."

"How long has he—" Nathan faltered. This wasn't any of his business.

"Lived with us?" Lisa didn't appear offended. "He

moved in when I was nine, and he's been with us ever since."

He wanted to ask about her real father but didn't have the guts. Besides, what did it matter? Charlie was the dad in her life, and that was what counted.

"We're ready to trim the tree," Nathan's father called from the top of the basement stairs.

Upstairs, Nathan's mother had set out a tray of hot chocolate and warm cookies and a large bowl of popcorn. A fire crackled in the fireplace, and boxes of beautiful decorations flanked the tree, now aglow with ribbons of tiny white lights. Christmas carols played on the audio system.

Karen stayed busy decorating the mantel with pine branches, silk magnolias, candles and a platoon of glass and china angels. Craig sat on the floor, gobbling cookies and untangling light strings for the stair banister.

"Your house looks like a still-life painting," Lisa whispered to Nathan. They stood together trimming the tree. "You do this *every* year?"

"For as long as I can remember. Don't you put up a tree every year?"

"Sure. Just not like this."

She didn't elaborate, and he was left to wonder what her Christmases had been like.

From one of the boxes, Lisa picked out an obviously homemade ornament—a Styrofoam ball thick with flaking gold glitter. "Your craft project?"

Before Nathan could say a word, his mother yelled,

91

"Don't drop that!" She rushed across the room, seizing the ball from Lisa's hands and cradling it tenderly in her own.

"I—I'm sorry," Lisa stammered.

Karen looked flustered. "I didn't mean to yell. It's just that this one has special meaning for me. I-it was made by someone special." She hung it reverently on the highest branch she could reach.

Lisa sidled Nathan a look of understanding, then offered, "If you really want to preserve it, maybe you should buy one of those special cases used for showing off baseballs. They can be sealed airtight, and that will really keep the ornament from falling apart. And I noticed a drawing on your refrigerator. It can be laminated, and that will keep it from falling apart too."

Nathan saw by his mother's expression that she had never thought of these things. She was stuck in a time warp about Molly and couldn't see the obvious. "Good ideas," he said. "Don't you think so, Mom?"

"Yes," Karen said stiffly. "I'll look into your suggestions."

When the tree was fully decorated, they stood around it, admired it, and sipped hot chocolate. Nathan had hoped to have Lisa stay and watch a movie with him, but once the tree was complete, she asked him to drive her home. "It was nice to meet you," Karen told Lisa, but her voice held none of the warmth Lisa's mother's had held when she first met Nathan.

He drove her home, nervous about saying good

night because he wanted to kiss her in the worst way. He pulled in next to Charlie's truck, but before he could turn off his engine, she jumped out of the car. "I had a good time."

"Hey, wait up. I'll go with you."

"No. I think Charlie and Mom are asleep," she said, leaning into the passenger window. "I'll see you in school on Monday."

Confused, and burning with desire, Nathan watched her hurry up the walk. He just couldn't figure her out. They'd had a good time together. She wasn't one bit put off by his mother. Lisa's own family seemed nice enough, if unconventional, so he didn't think they were the problem. So what was it? What made Lisa run?

I stand and watch you from afar. I wish upon you, like a star. . . . The words of his own poem returned, and with it, all the confused longing he'd felt the night he'd first written it. "Still, I love you better than you know," he said aloud, and swore to himself he would get inside her heart. Somehow.

"Did you have a good time?" Lisa's mother asked when Lisa let herself into the apartment. She was sitting on the worn sofa, scratching off silver finishes from a stack of lottery tickets.

"Mom, why do you waste your money this way?"

"Simple—if I don't play, I can't win. When I strike it rich, you and Charlie both will be eating your words. Now tell me about your dinner at Nathan's."

"I had a great time."

"Well, he's cute as can be and he sure seems nice."

"He is nice."

"And his family?"

"They're nice too, although I don't think his mother likes me."

Jill sank against the sofa. "That's crazy. Why wouldn't she like you?"

"Just a feeling."

"Have you—" Jill faltered. "You know . . . said anything to him yet?"

"I'm not going to do that."

"I don't get why you're so secretive. It's nothing to be ashamed of."

"Mom, please don't lecture me. You all agreed to let me play by my own rules."

"Yes, but—"

Just then Charlie came into the room. "Let her be, Jill. She knows what she wants."

Jill's expression turned sour, and she scraped furiously at another ticket.

Charlie handed Lisa a piece of paper. "Your call came Wednesday. I didn't tell you until now because I wanted you to have a good holiday. You're set up for two-thirty, five days a week."

"Two-thirty! But that means I'll have to leave school at one-thirty, and for weeks I'll miss half of the only class I really like."

"Your teacher will understand. If you have a problem, I'll speak to him."

"Fuller knows already." Lisa struggled against the lump in her throat. "I—I just thought I'd have more time to be normal."

Charlie squeezed her shoulder. "I'm sorry, baby girl."

Lisa fought back tears, pushed past him, and went to her room. She didn't want to cry. Not over something no amount of tears could ever change.

12

*F*uller never looked up from his lecture notes the first day that Lisa walked out of his class a half hour early. All eyes in the room watched her, including Nathan's, and although Lisa had been polite to him in the halls, she acted as if Friday night had never happened. Every time he looked at the Christmas tree, he saw her carefully hanging ornaments and smiling at him. She'd had a good time, he was sure of it; but now she had returned to her cool, elusive self. She was still a dream he chased.

On Friday, he caught up with Jodie and Skeet holding hands in the hallway and asked Jodie if she knew what was going on with Lisa.

"She doesn't confide in me," Jodie told him, her expression sympathetic.

"I thought you were friends."

"We are, up to a point. She's nice to me, but she keeps to herself. Sorry, Nathan."

"Will she bring you to practice tomorrow?"

"My mom's dropping me. She doesn't have to work this Saturday, and she wants to hear me sing. She won't stay long. That's all right, isn't it?"

"Sure. Yeah. Whatever." Nathan's pent-up frustration almost got the best of him. "Sooner or later I'm going to figure it out," he said stubbornly.

"I hope you do," Jodie said. "And when you do, will you tell us? I can't figure Lisa out either."

The Saturday practice went well, although Nathan's heart wasn't in it. He missed Lisa's presence and kept wondering where she was and what she was doing. And who she might be doing it with. That line of thinking had come about because of his mother's questioning. The minute Nathan had appeared in the kitchen to grab breakfast, Karen had asked, "So, is Lisa coming by today?"

"I don't know." He stubbornly held out hope that she might stop by, since she knew they would be rehearsing.

"If she comes, will she be riding that motorcycle?"

"It's how she gets around, Mom." Of course, his mother had noticed Lisa in the garage on Saturdays, but she'd not connected Nathan's feelings for the girl until he'd brought her home for dinner, so now her motorcycle was an issue.

"I think motorcycles are very dangerous. It's a wonder her parents let her have one."

"Does this mean Abby and Audrey won't be getting matching cycles when they're sixteen?"

"Don't be impertinent."

"Well, don't rag on Lisa." He hunkered over his cereal bowl, willing his mother to let him eat in peace.

"Do you *like* this girl, Nathan?"

"I like her."

"As a girlfriend?"

"A guy can dream."

His mother looked exasperated. "I can't believe she's your type. There are so many nice girls out there."

He dropped his spoon with a clank into his now empty bowl. "What's my type, Mom? Have you already picked out the perfect girl for me?"

"Well, no . . . it's just that Lisa seems so . . ." She searched for words, and Nathan felt his blood pressure going up. "Well, so much more mature than other high school girls I've met."

"I'm seventeen! I know what I like, and it's not some Barbie type."

"It's not about your ages," Karen added hastily. "It's an attitude. A disposition. I don't know how to describe it."

"Well, then please don't." He stood, then dumped his bowl and utensils in the dishwasher.

"Nathan, I'm not your enemy."

He grimaced.

"I care about you. The wrong girl at this time in your life could be disastrous. Lisa's pretty and she's sophisticated. Just because you two may be the same age, and in the same grade in high school, doesn't mean she's on the same wavelength as you. Why, she's probably dating much older boys. I—I just don't want to see you get hurt."

He exited the kitchen with his mother's words running around in his brain, and now, hours later, the words were still wedged there. Hadn't Skeet told him months ago that Lisa went out with college guys? Hadn't he known her reputation all along? Why would she even give a second look at a dork like Nathan? Yet the kiss he'd taken from her hounded him. She'd returned his kiss. Their mouths had fairly sizzled with it. And she'd treated him with a kind of tenderness that defied her hard-boiled image.

"Hey, Nate! You listening?" Skeet's voice jarred him out of his mind game.

Startled, Nathan looked up, somewhat surprised that he still was standing in his garage. "Sorry," he mumbled. "Tell me again."

"Larry has gotten us an audition at the VFW in Doraville, for a Christmas party. You think we're ready to tackle a whole evening of music for a live audience?"

Nathan looked from face to face of his band. Each looked excited, expectant, waiting for him to decide. A dance party for old codgers wasn't exactly the Grand Ole Opry.

"It pays," Larry said. "Not a fortune, but money's money."

"It's a place to start," Jodie offered.

"And the crowd may be hard of hearing, which couldn't hurt," Skeet joked.

Nathan shrugged. "Why not? Set it up."

Skeet, Larry and Jodie passed around high fives. "I've already given them an audition tape," Larry said. "That's why they asked us. They'll be printing up letters for the membership and want to know what we call ourselves. Any suggestions? We've got to have a name."

After a few minutes of reflection, Nathan said, "How about The Heartbreakers?"

The others tested it aloud. "Works for me," Skeet said, throwing his arm around Jodie. "We can always change it later if we want."

Nathan agreed.

Nathan was never certain when the idea to follow Lisa came to him. It just did. He rejected it at first. *Juvenile. Stupid. Boneheaded.* But another week of watching Lisa pick up and leave class early set him on the path to see what was going on with her for himself. He chose Friday as the day to do it, skipping Fuller's class altogether and waiting in the parking lot for her to emerge from the school building and climb onto her cycle. He'd never ditched a day of school in his life—mostly because homeschooling gave him plenty of freedom and he'd never needed to—but things were different now.

He sat hunched behind the wheel of his car and only straightened a little when Lisa appeared half a parking lot away. She snapped on her helmet, took off with a roar. He eased his car out of the lot and onto the street, careful to stay well behind her and keeping traffic in between. "You're pathetic, Malone," he said out loud, annoyed that he'd been reduced to a common sneak, but he didn't turn back.

He watched her pink helmet bob as she wove in and out of moving cars. She turned into a large parking garage and he crept inside once she was well out of sight. He'd been concentrating so hard on keeping up with her that he didn't know exactly where he was—just near some large buildings. To be safe, he drove up to the uppermost level and found a space. He looked around. The place was totally generic, with no signs to indicate anything except floor level and section. Cautiously he emerged from his car, crossed to a bank of elevators. He rode down with a group of strangers, stepped out when they did and was surprised to see himself inside a hospital lobby.

Lisa went to a *hospital* every day? That didn't make sense. The place looked mammoth. The atrium soared above him, and sunlight pouring through skylights turned the area yellow gold. A giant decorated Christmas tree filled up one corner of the lobby near a gift boutique.

"May I help you, young man? You look lost."

He turned to see an information desk and an elderly woman dressed in a pink uniform. "I—I'm not sure," he said, walking over.

"Are you here to see a particular doctor? Perhaps have testing done?"

"I—um—was supposed to meet a friend here, but I can't remember where she said to meet her." The lies were falling easily off his tongue, so Nathan forged ahead.

"Well, if the person's come for day surgery—"

"No. I don't think so. She comes every day, though."

The woman looked thoughtful. "Perhaps chemo-therapy. Or maybe dialysis. But that's usually every other day. Radiation is a possibility. How long has she been coming?"

Every word fell like hammer blows on Nathan's heart. He backpedaled. "You know, I passed her car in the parking garage. I'll just wait for her there."

The woman smiled, gave her attention to another man who had stepped up to her desk.

Nathan retreated to the garage, his heart pounding. Was Lisa sick? He thought about it. She didn't look sick. She never acted sick. Why would she come here every day? A job? He could handle that. He'd known a girl who was a teen volunteer at a hospital. She had wanted to be a doctor. But why would Lisa be so secretive about a volunteer job?

There *had* to be an explanation. Maybe she was seeing a psychiatrist. That would be ironic, because he was the one acting nuts! And people didn't see shrinks every day, if he remembered correctly. All at once, he was out of conjectures. He would have to find her cycle in the huge garage, wait for her, and confront her. Humiliating as it would be, asking her was the only way to *really* know.

A big black cycle with a painted red heart was easier to spot than a specific car, and Nathan found her Harley two floors below where he had parked. He wished he'd worn his watch, but he hadn't, so he wasn't sure how long he waited, but eventually, he heard the click of boot heels on concrete coming closer.

He was leaning against the concrete wall in front of her cycle when she saw him. She blinked, confused over seeing him out of context.

He stepped forward. "Hi, Lisa."

"How did you—"

His cheeks flamed red. Suddenly, revelation seemed to wash over her. "Did you *follow* me?"

"Yes," he said softly. "I have to know why you leave school early and come here every day."

Impulsively, she swore at him, adding hotly, "Who do you think you are? What gives you the *right* to follow me?"

"I took the right." Nathan stepped closer until he was almost nose to nose with her. "I took it because . . . because, you see . . . I love you."

13

*H*is confession sounded so anguished, his expression looked so vulnerable, that Lisa was reminded of the glass angels on his fireplace mantel. With the right well-chosen words, she could break him, and now was the time to do it if she was ever going to be free of him. *Except...* Emotion clogged her throat, moisture filmed her vision, blurring his face, turning his features shimmery. She whispered, "That makes no sense. You hardly know me."

Nathan watched Lisa's eyes fill with tears. He touched her cheek, fully expecting her to shove him backward. He wasn't sorry for what he'd said. He *did* love her. "It's not about *knowing,* Lisa. It's about *feeling.* Believe me, I wish I didn't feel the way I do about you. I think about you all the time—first thing in the morning. Last thing at night."

She seemed to crumble from the inside out. Her shoulders heaved and he took her slowly into his arms, pressed his cheek against her thick dark hair, let her cry hard and long. If he could have stretched the minutes into eternity, he would have; he wished they could be someplace else, anywhere other than a cold, lonely hospital parking garage. Cars circled past them, but no one seemed to notice them. Nathan was glad for that.

When her sobs lessened, Nathan stroked her hair, lifted her chin. She was beginning to shiver from the cold, and her whole body trembled.

"Don't look at me," she said. "Crying makes me look awful."

"Not to me." He had no tissue to offer her. "My car's up a couple of floors. Let me take you someplace warmer. Want some coffee?"

"My ride . . . ," she said, looking at her cycle.

"I'll bring you back for it."

He was amazed when she didn't argue. He took her to his car, got her tucked inside, turned on the heater full blast and slowly wound his way down to the street level. There he got his bearings, drove to the closest coffee shop and walked her inside. The shop had an empty sofa in a corner, so he settled her there, bought them both steaming cups of fresh coffee and sat next to her so that he was touching her. "Talk to me," he said.

Her hands were icy cold, and she warmed them around the cup. He wanted explanations, and she was loathe to give them. Her opportunity to cut and run had passed and she knew it. "I'll tell you everything."

Her voice held the raspy sound of weeping. "Just not right now. I—I need some time to pull it all together in my head."

He was disappointed, but he sensed a change in her, a difference that he hoped wouldn't disappear. He told himself to be patient. "Tell me when and where," he said.

"Come to my apartment later. Mom's playing bingo tonight and Charlie will be out with some of his friends."

"What time?"

"After seven."

"And you promise to be there?"

"I'll be there."

"And you'll let me in?"

A tiny smile crept into her heart over his distrust. She knew he was already *in.* "I'll let you in."

Nathan was cheerful at dinner that night, making conversation without his parents' having to pry things out of him. He offered snippets from his day, omitting his ditching adventure without even a qualm of conscience. All he could focus on was getting out of the house and going to be with Lisa. He cleared the table and loaded the dishwasher quickly, and as soon as his mother reappeared from bathing the twins, he announced that he and Skeet were headed to the mall and a movie.

He had been on rocky ground with his mother for a week, their discussion about Lisa standing like a wall between them. Nathan was glad she didn't give him her usual third degree when he went out—he could recite her line of questions from memory—and he was grateful for the break. He was also grateful that his father had been working long hours at his office and hadn't been sucked into the mother-son conflict.

Nathan drove to Lisa's, parked in front of her building, went to her door and knocked. He felt great relief when she opened the door.

"I made us popcorn," she said. "You want a cola?"

He did. The place was lit by two lamps, and from the back hall he heard the television. "Um—how are you feeling?"

She gave him a funny look. "I feel fine, Malone."

For a minute he thought she might have reverted to her old ways. "Me too," he said.

That made her smile. "Want to see my room?"

"Seems fair. I showed you mine."

Lisa's room was especially large, with a bathroom on one end and a wall of closet doors on the other. He realized it was really the apartment's master bedroom, which made him wonder why she'd gotten it instead of her mother and Charlie. "Nice," he said, panning the room, taking in everything at once.

His gaze rested on the room's focal point, a photographic mural of treetops filled with fiery red blossoms. It ran the length of the room's longest wall, across from a quilt-covered queen-size bed, which was under a window and heaped with decorative pillows. There was a desk, no computer, floor pillows, and a short bookcase stuffed with books and CDs. He walked to the mural, touched the paper and its crimson flowers. "Looks real."

"It's the tops of royal poincianas—flame trees," Lisa said from behind him. "When we lived in Miami, there was one in our backyard, and every spring it put out these incredible red-orange flowers. I loved it. I used to have tea parties under it. The tree's leaves are very tiny, so when I stood under it and there was any kind of breeze, the shadow patterns looked like lace on my skin, and I felt like a princess. The branches grow up really high and form a canopy, like an umbrella. When I was a kid, I thought it would one day touch the sky, and then I planned to climb up it and touch the sky too." Lisa ran her palm along the mural, caressing the paper flowers as she talked.

"It's a pretty tree," he said, more fascinated by Lisa's descriptions and revelations than by the mural. "I've never seen one before."

"They don't grow this far north. I wish they did." She cast a longing look at the photograph.

Nathan didn't get her attachment, but then he didn't understand his mother's obsessive interest in their backyard either. "I've got to admit, it's kind of a different look for a bedroom."

"What did you expect to see? Posters of rock stars?"

"I've learned not to have expectations when it comes to you, Lisa."

She arched an eyebrow, thrust the bowl of popcorn at him. He took a handful, went to her bed and began to sort through pillows. "Quite a collection." They were in all sizes and shapes. Some looked like animals, others were richly decorated with tassels, braids and beads. One was shaped and decorated like a motorcycle.

"My mother gives them to me. She likes to shop and add to my stash. I don't know what I'm going to do with all of them when I—"

She stopped so abruptly, Nathan was caught off guard. Her face looked flushed. "When you what?"

"Leave. You know, move on."

He wasn't sure that was what she'd meant to say.

"Give them away, I suppose," she said.

"Talk to me, Lisa." Nathan was growing impatient for her to move into the real reason he'd come over.

She tossed him a floor pillow and settled cross-legged onto another, then put the popcorn bowl between them. She looked nervous, not at all like her usual in-control self. "What do you want to know?"

"Duh. The hospital."

"It's a boring story."

"I've got all night."

"What, no curfew?"

"You're procrastinating."

"Yes, I am. On purpose. It's something I hate to talk about."

He sat perfectly still, watching the light play on her hair and cheekbones. He wanted to lay her down and kiss her.

"When I was eleven, almost twelve, I started having

bad headaches. I began seeing double, staggering and falling down for no reason. We lived in Miami then. Me and Mom and Charlie." She stared over Nathan's head as she spoke.

"Your real dad?"

"Not part of the picture. He was long gone."

"Go on."

"We had a little house in North Miami. There was a yard and my tree. I had school and friends."

"And headaches," Nathan said, reminding her of the original tack.

"I was put in a hospital. I had all kinds of tests—lots of needles and big scary-looking machines aimed at me. God, I hated it so much." She shuddered. "In the end, they told us I had a brain stem glioma." She paused. "*Glioma.* It's a pretty word, don't you think?"

His heart pounded with increasing dread. "If you say so."

"But it's not a pretty thing, Malone. No, glioma isn't pretty at all." She looked at the mural of the trees. "It's a kind of brain tumor. Most are malignant, and so was mine. It was growing in my upper cerebellum." She clamped a hand to the base of her neck. "You remember what the cerebellum does from biology class, don't you?"

He tried to nod.

"Refresher course." She held up a finger. "It coordinates body movements and lies next to the brain stem, which controls breathing and heartbeats and swallowing.

My little glioma cells were slow growing—a good thing, but also very stubborn ... as in hard to kill." She plucked at the fringe on her floor pillow while she talked. "They couldn't do surgery: the tumor was too close to the brain stem. Chemo doesn't affect the type of cancer I had. That left radiation. So, they mapped out a field on my neck, marked it with small permanent blue dots."

She lifted her hair, turned so that he could see the dots. He'd seen them before and recalled thinking they might have been part of a tattoo she'd decided against. Now he saw that they were laid out in a grid pattern, and more marks had been added. Her hair had been cut too, shaved up the back of her neck and into the base of her skull. The outer layer of hair had been left alone, and it covered the marks and the shaved area when it hung loose. He wanted to touch her neck, trace his fingers along the path. "I see them."

She let go and her hair fell like a curtain over the telltale grid. "I went for treatments five days a week, for many weeks. Radiation doesn't hurt; it makes you tired, though. I was pretty scared. I had to lie really still with this monster machine aimed at my neck and the grid. The room had a large glass window and I could see my radiologist, Dr. Glickman, and Charlie from the table. Charlie called the machine a zapper because it was going to zap and destroy the bad cells. He said it was like a video game, and I understood that because he and I would play Nintendo for hours and every time either of us made a kill, Charlie said that was just like the radiation treatments killing my cancer cells."

"It must have worked," Nathan said. "You're here."

"It worked. To a degree. They never said I would be cured. Just that the best we could hope for was halting the growth for a time. Most people with brain cancer live two to five years after treatments, if they're lucky. I've made it six."

Nathan's heart was pounding so hard, he thought it would pop from his chest. He tasted bile. "Meaning?"

"It's growing again."

14

*N*athan was reeling. Lisa had a brain tumor. The look on her face was open and guileless, her violet eyes, clear and pure. How could such a terrible thing be happening to someone so young and beautiful? "What are the doctors doing for you now?"

"Radiation again. I go five days a week."

That explained her leaving school early and the hospital visits. "Haven't they figured out some other way to treat this thing by now?"

"Not yet."

Her answer upset him. What had medical science been doing for all this time? What about all the cancer research he'd heard about, even read about? Why couldn't any of it help Lisa? "What about in other cities? Other countries?"

"Atlanta has a renowned cancer treatment center. Some of the best doctors in the world are here."

"And they still only use *radiation?*"

"I won't do experimental treatments."

"But why not? If it will help?"

"I don't know if they will help. Most don't, according to research. Gliomas are . . . well, just a bitch to deal with. And . . . and it's not the way I want to spend what's left of my life, hopping from one experiment to another. In and out of hospitals. Feeling like crap." She smiled ruefully. "I'd rather live like I was dying, not die without ever living."

"And your mom and Charlie are letting you *do* this?" Nathan couldn't believe what he was hearing. His mother would have tied him down and made him try every medical hope out there if the same thing were happening to him.

"I'm eighteen, Malone. I can do what I want. And they let me have control. I don't *have* to finish high school, you know. It's kind of silly in a way. But I want to graduate. For some dumb reason, I really do."

Subdued, he asked, "Is the radiation working? Is the tumor shrinking like last time?"

"Too soon to tell."

"But it probably will. I mean, the radiation worked before."

She tossed a kernel of popcorn at him. "Hey, Malone, don't freak out on me. It is what it is."

He jumped up, started pacing. "Well, it sucks! Big-time."

Lisa stood up too. "Now listen to me. There are

some rules for you that go along with this information I just dumped on you."

"What rules?"

"You can't tell anyone about this. Not Skeet, not anyone. You hear me?"

"Why?"

"Because I won't have that whole school staring at me and whispering about me every time I walk down the hall."

"But—"

"Would *you* want Roddy and his little friends making fun of *you*?"

"They wouldn't—"

"Oh please! Grow up. I went through it before. At my other school, kids acted like I had the plague. Half the middle school wouldn't come near me. Some even did gimp imitations . . . you know, dragging their leg and scrunching up their faces like a Frankenstein monster."

"They made *fun* of you? That's sick."

"The shrink I saw at the time said—and now I'm quoting: 'It's how they cope with their own fears about getting cancer themselves.' So what? It didn't make it hurt any less."

"But this is high school. Don't you think people might have matured by now?"

She crossed her arms. "Do you? Some of the 'mature ones' make oinking sounds whenever Jodie walks past. You saw for yourself how they go after Skeet for no known reason. I don't want them to know one thing about me. You got that?"

Of course, he understood, but he still couldn't get over it. Apparently homeschooling had shielded him from a lot of things. "So no one but me knows about you?"

"Fuller knows."

Nathan said, "And Charlie and your mother."

"They've lived with it for a long time. I'm almost glad the waiting is over. It was like waiting for the other shoe to fall because—" Her voice caught and she looked away. His heart squeezed, but he waited for her to finish. "Because we always knew it would come back. And now it has."

It explained a lot to Nathan. Her recklessness and in-your-face attitude. Her disdain of school cliques and rules she didn't like. Her refusal to let anyone get close to her. Lisa had chosen *not* to care because it protected her from hurtful things she thought were far worse than cancer. Nathan got something else too. By allowing Lisa to handle what was happening to her, and by giving her the freedom to come and go as she pleased, her mother and Charlie kept her with them. "I'll keep your secret," he said.

"I mean it. If this gets out, I'll leave this place so fast . . ." She let the implications sink in.

Nathan moved closer, so close he could feel the heat from her body. "What I said earlier, about loving you . . . this doesn't change anything."

She looked incredulous. "I have cancer, Malone. Go find a normal girl."

"I don't care. I love you, Lisa. And I'm not splitting. Get used to it."

Nathan watched Lisa leave Fuller's class every day, and his heart ached because he knew where she was going. He gritted his teeth when he heard others in their class call her "Diva" or speculate on what she might be doing with Fuller on the side for the privilege of walking out each day. Nathan wanted to hurt them. They were stupid. Mean and stupid. He couldn't wait for the Christmas holidays to come, because he swore to himself that he would spend every free minute with her.

"Where's your head, man?" Skeet asked at practices. "This gig is next Saturday and you're off in la-la land. We need you here, with us."

"Sorry," Nathan mumbled, and forced himself to concentrate on the music.

Lisa rarely came to rehearsals, which they had increased to include three afternoons a week. When she did visit, she sat in the shadows. He was careful not to look her way if Skeet went off on him, because he knew she'd think it was her fault.

"Do you *get* that these guys are paying us *money* to be good?" Skeet said. "And that if they like us, it can lead to other gigs?"

"I said I was sorry. Let's start again."

The worst was his mother's prying. "What's *wrong* with you?" she demanded one night at the dinner table.

"Nothing."

"Don't tell me that. It's like you've crawled into some dark cave. If school is too much for you—"

"What's too much for me is the way you hound me."

"Don't talk to your mother like that," his father ordered.

Their loud voices started Abby crying in her high chair. Seconds later Audrey joined in. "Now look what you've done," his mother snapped. She offered each girl a teething ring.

His father, the peacemaker, said, "Nate, I've talked to my boss and they're making a place for you in the mailroom for the time you're out of school over the holidays."

"Thanks, but no thanks. I don't want to work over the holidays."

"What! I went to bat for you, son. They're doing this as a favor for me."

"Dad, I'm sorry, but not this year."

"You said you needed the money."

"I'm making a little cash with the band for two parties."

"Money you'll have to split four ways. What's the matter with you? Why are you acting this way?"

Nathan didn't answer. He stood, wadded his paper napkin. "I'm finished with supper. I've got a big paper to do."

"Don't walk away from this table," his mother shouted.

Abby wailed and threw down her teething ring, and Audrey followed suit. Nathan kept moving.

"If this place was any dorkier, we could register it." The comment came from Larry as the band was setting up on the stage of the VFW in Doraville.

The room was old, tired-looking, with cheap paneled walls, long tables and metal chairs, and an open area around a dusty stage for dancing. Tinsel had been taped on the walls, along with Happy Holidays signs, and gaudy decorations hung on an artificial tree that had seen better days. The American flag, along with banners and photos of VFW members, covered another wall.

"You'll feel better when they pay us," Skeet said, flexing his fingers and running chords on his keyboard.

"Did you see the guy who let us in? He's older than God. I just hope nobody keels over dead tonight," Larry said.

"I'm like, *so* nervous," Jodie said. She was wearing jeans and a red shirt with some sequins sewn on the collar and cuffs.

"You'll be great, babe," Skeet said.

Nathan said nothing. He tuned his guitar and watched the door. Lisa had promised she would come. The event was scheduled to start in forty-five minutes and she hadn't shown up, but there was plenty of time.

An elderly man came up to the stage and introduced himself as the president of the group. "You *can* play the old ones, can't you? The *good* country songs?"

"Jodie here sounds just like Patsy Cline," Nathan said, his gaze on the door.

"Yes, we like Patsy. And Loretta and Reba too. Real country, you know."

"We won't let you down," Skeet said.

The room began to fill with elderly couples, and the tables grew crowded. The smell of barbecue drifted from the kitchen. At some point the band was introduced, and Nathan and his friends began to play. They were tight and nervous at first, but once Jodie got over her butterflies, they hit a groove and their sound mellowed out. Couples actually began to dance to the music. Everything would have been perfect except that Lisa never arrived. Nathan gave up watching the door and got into the music, torn between loving her and loathing her for jerking him around.

By ten o'clock the guests were gone, and The Heartbreakers were packing up their gear. Skeet said, "This didn't last long. Maybe we can play to a younger crowd next time."

"The next one's a birthday party with a Western theme," Larry said. "The guy's turning forty."

"Not much better."

Jodie took a swig from a soda. "It's all right with me. I got to sing."

"Like an angel," Skeet said. "You all want to grab some burgers? I'm starved."

Larry and Jodie agreed enthusiastically.

Nathan was in no mood for socializing. He pushed outside, carrying two guitar cases and a box with a special mike for his acoustical guitar, and headed for his car.

"How'd it go, cowboy?" The question came from Lisa. She was wrapped in a long suede coat and leaning against her bike.

Nathan's heart leaped with pleasure at the sight of her. He brushed past her, determined not to let her know. How could she stand there so nonchalant, as if she hadn't known how important their very first paid engagement was to them? "You're a little late for the party."

"I'm here to make it up to you. Hop on. I have another party for us to catch."

He wanted to say, *Forget it*. He wanted to blow her off the way she'd done to him.

"Hey, Lisa." Jodie came up and hugged her friend. "We were great! Sorry you missed it."

"I'll bet you were."

Not a word of apology, Nathan thought, but even as he thought it, he locked his gear in his trunk and handed Skeet the keys. "Go on without me."

"You sure?"

"Park at your house. Like last time." Nathan got onto Lisa's bike; she handed him a helmet and started the engine. He settled into the hard leather seat, angry at himself for not being stronger and walking away. Furious. But it didn't matter. Nothing mattered except being with Lisa. Nothing.

15

"Where are we going?" Nathan shouted above the road noise and the sound of the Harley's engine.

"Fraternity row at Tech."

Nathan wasn't sure he liked the idea of hitting a party at Georgia Tech, but he didn't want to argue with her. She could have gone without him, but she hadn't.

By the time she parked her cycle on the lawn of a fraternity house, Nathan was cold and not in a great mood. Light poured from every window of the old house, music blared out to the sidewalk, and people spilled onto the lawn in drunken groups. Lisa headed inside and Nathan followed. The smell of booze was strong, and Lisa wasted no time in grabbing them both bottles of beer. "Drink up," she said, tipping her bottle upward.

Nathan took a sip from his.

"Hey, Lisa, baby! Long time no see." A guy came up from behind them and swooped Lisa up in his arms. "Where have you been, sweet thing?"

"Around. There are other places to party, you know." She pulled away, nodded toward Nathan. "Meet a friend of mine."

The guy glanced toward Nathan. "Any friend of Lisa's . . ."

"I got it."

"You looking over the Greeks?"

"Not yet," Nathan said.

"Well, this is party central. If you're into partying, that is." He put his arm around Lisa's waist. "And if you're with Lisa, you *got* to be into partying." He kissed her cheek, and she shooed him away.

"What?" Lisa said to Nathan, looking irritated.

"Why are you doing this? To show me how cool you are?" He was angry at her and jealous of every guy she had a past with.

"Life's short." She turned on her heel and melded into the crowd.

Her words stung. Nathan elbowed his way behind her, caught up with her just as she was heading to dance with some other guy who was nuzzling her neck. Nathan watched and seethed. If she was trying to hurt him, she was succeeding. He didn't think the song would ever end, and when it did, he shoved through and caught her up under his arm. "Wondered where you got off to." He told the guy, "I use the head and next thing you know, I'm dateless. But now I'm here to take her off your hands."

The guy, who looked glassy-eyed, gave a drunken shrug and staggered off. Lisa said, "Don't go possessive on me, Malone."

The music screamed around them. All he wanted to do was get her out of there.

"I need another beer," she said.

"Take mine."

She held it against her temple and Nathan saw perspiration prickling her upper lip. Her skin looked pale and clammy, and she was trembling.

"Come with me." Shielding her, he wove them both through the room to the front door and outside into the chilly night air. She stumbled. He led her across the lawn and away from others. "What's wrong?" He didn't figure she'd had enough beer to be drunk, but something was definitely going on with her.

"Go away," she said. She dropped the bottle, staggered behind a hedge of bushes, and fell to her knees. He heard her vomiting. He plowed through the brush and knelt beside her. "What can I do?"

"Nothing." Her face was contorted with pain.

"Let me help you."

She pressed the heels of her hands into her eyes. "Bad headache."

Nathan's gut seized. "Just lie down." She needed no urging. He ripped off his jacket and made a pillow for her head. He remembered that she'd stuffed her long coat into a saddlebag on her cycle. "I'll be right back." He raced to where they'd left the Harley, quickly pushed it to where she was lying. He could hear her moaning. He fumbled in the saddlebag, grabbed her coat and covered her. "Tell me what to do."

"Nothing . . . to . . . do . . . ," she managed.

He couldn't watch her suffer. He rummaged through the bags, pulling out lipstick, a hairbrush and then her cell phone. He found Charlie's preprogrammed number, punched it. When Charlie answered, Nathan said, "Lisa's sick. We need help."

Nathan held Lisa, smoothing her hair and rocking her until Charlie's pickup arrived at the curb. "Over here!" Nathan shouted. Charlie ran over, scooped up Lisa as if she were a small child, walked her to the truck and laid her on the front seat. "Help me with the cycle," he said to Nathan.

Together, they lifted the machine into the bed of the pickup and Charlie swiftly secured it. "It happened so fast," Nathan said. "One minute we were dancing. The next she was in horrible pain."

"Sit up front and hold her while I drive," Charlie said.

Nathan did as he was told, all the while his heart hammering with fear. Lisa moaned. "She'll be all right, won't she?"

"She needs to go to the ER. Morphine's the only thing that helps when the headaches are this bad."

Charlie made record time on the freeway, pulled into the semicircle parking in front of the emergency room at Grady Hospital reserved for ambulances, and lifted Lisa from Nathan's arms. "Park the truck. Meet me inside."

By the time Nathan found a space and went inside, Charlie was filling out paperwork in an area crammed with waiting patients. He said, "They took her into triage. They called her doctor. Nothing to do now except wait."

Charlie turned in the paperwork, returned to the chair Nathan held open for him. They sat side by side, Charlie looking at the floor, Nathan pushed back against the wall. After a few minutes, Nathan said, "How often does this happen to her?"

"The headaches come and go. No pattern. No warning."

"Does it mean the radiation isn't helping?"

Charlie glanced over at Nathan. "She's told you about that?"

"Yes."

"That's good. I told her she should."

"It stinks. Her being sick and all."

"It does," Charlie said. "Things went pretty good for a long time. We almost forgot the tumor would grow again." Charlie's use of *we* made Nathan aware that Lisa's mother hadn't shown up. He wondered about it, but didn't know how to ask. "If you need to leave—"

"Not until I know she's okay," Nathan told him, aware that he was way past his curfew, and not caring.

"It could take a while."

"I'll wait."

At some point, a doctor appeared and talked to Charlie. When he left, Charlie said, "They're going to keep her for observation."

"When can she leave?"

"Probably tomorrow. We can go back and see her, though."

A nurse in green scrubs led them to a curtained-off area. Lisa was on a bed, eyes closed. An IV line was taped to her arm, and the tubing ran to a bag of clear liquid hooked to a pole. To Nathan, she looked child-like, as pale as paste, as fragile as bone china. All he wanted to do was hold her.

Charlie bent and kissed her forehead. "Hey, princess."

Her eyelids fluttered open. "It was a bad one, Charlie." She looked drugged and her speech slurred. She focused on Nathan, her expression confused. "Why are you here?"

"Don't you remember the party?"

"Sort of. I got sick."

"From the pain," he clarified, forgiving her everything.

"You should have gone home. You'll get in trouble."

"And miss this adventure? No way."

Her eyelids drooped. "Keep . . . my . . . secret, Malone."

Once she was asleep, Charlie said, "I'll take you home, Nathan." Everyone seemed to call him by his first name but Lisa. "I'll talk to your parents if you want me to."

"I'll handle it," Nathan said.

They left the ER.

Nathan made no pretense of sneaking into his house. He went into the kitchen and to the refrigerator. From a chair at the table, his mother raised up like an apparition. "You are so grounded, mister."

"Okay," Nathan said. He extracted a cola, shut the door, popped the tab.

"Is that all you have to say for yourself?" She snapped on the overhead light. "Where *were* you? Do you know what time it is?"

He glanced at the clock, saw that it was after four in the morning, thought better of telling her the obvious, and took a long drink from his cola. "I went to a party with Lisa."

"Without permission?"

"Call me wild and crazy."

Karen came closer. "Don't be flip. Why didn't you call? I've left a dozen messages on your cell phone. I've been worried sick!"

In truth, he'd forgotten about his cell phone. "I turned it off while our band played tonight and forgot to turn it back on. Sorry."

"Oh, please!" She stomped to the counter. "Did you ride on that girl's cycle?"

"We did." He knew she wouldn't have asked if she didn't already know the answer.

"Skeet said you had."

"You called Skeet?"

"What was I supposed to do? You weren't home and I could see your car in his driveway."

"Hope you don't get him in trouble. You know how his old man is."

"That's your fault too." She banged her fist on the cold granite top.

"I'd like to go to bed now."

She glared at him. "Sleep fast because there are some new rules. You *will* be going to work today and every day of your school break with your father. You *will* come home with him and go nowhere else. You hear me?"

He wanted to protest, but knew that it would be useless at the moment. She was mad and needed time to cool off. He also knew that there was no way he was going to remain under house arrest for two weeks. One way or another, he was going to see Lisa over the holidays.

"You want to talk about it?" Nathan's father asked as they drove into work the next morning.

"No." Nathan's eyes were closed, and he had tipped the passenger's seat as far back as it would go. Three hours of sleep had done him more harm than good.

"Why do you go out of your way to provoke her, son?"

"I don't mean to."

"But you know her hot buttons and lately it seems

like you make up new ways to push them." They rode in silence before his father said, "Is this girl *this* important to you?"

Nathan raised his head. "Yes. She is."

His father's jaw tightened. "You be careful, all right?"

Nathan knew what his father was thinking, and he didn't need a lecture about safe sex at the moment. Nathan knew how to protect his body. He had no idea how to protect his heart. "I'll be careful," he said.

Nathan's father cut his eyes sideways. "Your mother loves you. You need to understand where she's coming from." In the parking garage, Craig turned off the engine but didn't move to get out of the car.

Now what? Nathan wondered.

"Do you remember anything about that day?"

Nathan didn't have to be a rocket scientist to know which day he was talking about—the day that had changed their lives forever. "You mean the day Molly died," he said.

16

"Why are you bringing this up now?" Nathan asked. He really didn't want to talk about it.

"I think it will help you see things from her—*our* perspective," his father said.

"Right now?" All Nathan wanted to do was go inside, get to work and call about Lisa.

Ignoring his question, his father continued. "We bought our house in late July, about three years after we were married. It was a big house and much more than we could afford, but your mother's grandfather had died and left her a small inheritance. That's what we used for the down payment. We figured we'd make the payments over the life of the mortgage somehow."

Nathan looked straight ahead as his father talked, at the cold cement wall of the parking garage, and wondered why earthshaking information seemed to be delivered to him in parking garages.

"One of the reasons your mom loved the house was because it had a pool. Did you know she was on her high school swim team?" His dad didn't wait for Nathan to reply. He plunged ahead. "Molly was especially excited about it, but neither of you could swim and we didn't want to be foolish, so we fenced in the pool and I installed a special latch up high where little fingers couldn't reach. Your mom wanted the two of you to learn from the best, so she hired a certified teacher for you and Molly."

"I don't remember."

"No reason you should. You were barely three. In September, Molly started first grade. You both had taken two lessons, but Molly was certain that she could swim. She threw tantrums when your mother made her wear water wings. She kept saying she was a 'big girl.' She didn't need them, only babies like Nathan needed them."

His father pinched the bridge of his nose wearily. Nathan wished he'd stop the story, yet knew he wouldn't, and worse, Nathan knew he should hear it. "You got sick," his dad explained. "Kids' stuff, ear infection, congestion. You were miserable and awake for about three nights in a row and your mom was awake with you. By Saturday, you were on an antibiotic and getting well. Best of all, you were sleeping again too. Molly was too old for naps, but we insisted on her having a quiet time in her room. I was out playing golf that day. Your mom was so tired that she lay down and fell sound asleep when you did."

Nathan's heart was racing now because he knew where the story was going, and it was making him sick to his stomach.

"Molly was a precocious child, such a smart, clever little girl. Once you and Mom were asleep, she sneaked out of her room, down the stairs. She even dragged a dining room chair to the gate and stood on it so she could reach the latch." He took a breath, and his voice took on a raspy quality. "And she got it open. Your room was overlooking the backyard at that time, and you must have seen her in the pool from your window because when Mom came into your room and asked if you knew where Molly was, you said, 'Molly go swim.'"

From the deepest recesses of his memory, Nathan heard a wailing sound. He wasn't sure if it was the sound of his mother's anguish or a siren. He shook his head to clear out the noise. In his mind, he saw a bird's-eye view of the backyard, a blue-water pool and someone floating facedown. *A memory?* Again, Nathan wasn't sure. Emotion clogged his throat and he couldn't speak.

"The paramedics came but couldn't do anything for her. Molly was dead. After the funeral, we hired a contractor to take out the pool. We put in gardens to remind ourselves that life goes on. I believe that everything your mother plants is a tribute to Molly's memory."

Nathan knew it was true.

"At any rate, your mother never forgave herself for falling asleep, and *you* became the focus of her life." His father squeezed Nathan's shoulder. "I know you want to grow up, son. I know you feel smothered sometimes. All I want you to realize is *why* she's this way and—and to be kind to her."

Nathan cleared his throat. "She shouldn't blame herself, Dad. It was an accident."

"We know that in our heads, but in our hearts—" He paused. "Well, in your heart you tell yourself you should have prevented it from happening. If she had lived, Molly would have graduated from high school by now, gone to college or gotten a job, maybe even gotten married. No way of ever knowing, of course. When a child dies, dreams die."

Nathan's insides turned cold. Lisa's face materialized on the concrete wall outside the car's windshield as his father's words went through him like a sword.

Going back to work at his dad's office in downtown Atlanta wasn't difficult for Nathan. Not only was he warmly greeted by his dad's colleagues, he had use of the company van for errands and deliveries, plus free time. The first opportunity, he called Lisa's cell and was relieved when she answered. She was home.

"Charlie told me how much you helped. Thanks for that. Did you get in much trouble?"

"Not too much."

"How did your gig go? I never asked you, and I

should have. I wanted to come, but the headache came on. I took some stuff and thought I'd knocked it out. I was wrong."

"We got paid, so they must have liked us." He paused. "Do you get headaches like that very often?"

"Please don't ask me questions about my health. I really don't like talking about it."

Didn't she understand how worried he was about her? Didn't she know that he couldn't simply forget what was happening to her? He didn't want to scare her off though, or have her retreat into her isolation mode, so he asked, "When can I see you?"

"Aside from radiation treatments, I'll be hanging around until school starts back up."

He told her about work and said he'd be sticking close to home evenings. "But we can meet for lunch when I have a delivery out your way."

She read between the lines. "I thought you said you weren't in trouble."

"Maybe just a little bit of trouble."

"I'll meet you wherever you want."

Nathan felt elated. "I'll let you know."

On Saturday, The Heartbreakers played at a man's fortieth birthday party. After dropping off Skeet and Jodie, Nathan fought the urge to go to Lisa's and instead went home like a good boy, arriving before the eleven-o'clock news. On Sunday afternoon, Nathan wheedled time out of his mother to go Christmas shopping at the mall. He bought toys for the twins, a sweater for his mother, a dress shirt for his dad and a video game for Skeet. He spent the bulk of his money on a heart-shaped necklace for Lisa. Two days before Christmas, he met her in one of the city's public parks and gave it to her. The day had turned blustery, the sky gray, but sitting on the park bench watching her unwrap his gift made him forget everything except being near her.

"It's beautiful," she said, holding it up to catch the light.

Like you, he wanted to say, but knew it would sound too corny. "Let me put it on you."

She stroked the gold heart once he snapped the catch. "I have something for you too." She reached into the oversize handbag she was carrying and pulled out two wrapped items. One was a CD of a hot country band. "You have it?"

He didn't. He unwrapped the other gift and discovered a book on how to market songs—how to sell music, and names and addresses of agents, houses and music industry labels.

"I haven't thought about selling my songs in a while."

"Why not? You can't forget your dreams."

"Pipe dreams."

"Has Fuller read any of your work out loud yet?"

"A couple." Nathan squirmed, not wanting her to know he'd written the one poem for her. Which didn't make sense because he'd all but laid his heart at her feet. "How about you? He read any of your stuff?"

"Some."

"Some is more than a couple."

"A figure of speech." She looked up at the low gray clouds blanketing the sky. "I wish it were spring."

"It's not too far away."

"Far enough," she said.

Right after Christmas, Nathan got the idea of inviting Lisa to his house. How could his mother object to that? They'd be right there under her watchful eye. Karen agreed, but Nathan saw by his mother's expression that she wasn't thrilled with the idea. What surprised him was that Lisa agreed to come. And she came often, making a guarded peace with his mother by talking about flowers and Lisa's beloved flame trees.

"I've never seen one," Karen confessed.

"Experts consider royal poincianas one of the most beautiful species of tree in the world," Lisa told her.

"I'll look it up on the Internet," Karen promised.

Lisa adored the twins, and they always smiled when they saw her face. Nathan told her, "I think Audrey really likes you. She's the shy one, and doesn't take to many people."

"They're really cute. You're lucky to have siblings."

"Huge age gap though. They'll give Mom something to do when I'm gone."

"She'll miss you."

"Don't think she hasn't mentioned it several hundred times. If she had her way, I'd live in this basement until I was an old man." Ever since his father's talk, Nathan anticipated his mother's protectiveness, but it hadn't made him like it any better. "How about your mom? She doesn't smother you."

Lisa looked thoughtful for a moment. "She's over the smothering stage. We have an understanding, remember? I appreciate her and everything, it's just that this isn't what she signed on for. You know, having a sick kid."

"That's not your fault."

"It doesn't matter. It's still a handicap. Mom wanted to travel, see the country, maybe even the world. She had plans for her and Charlie to get married and travel all over in an RV once I moved away."

"Why don't they get married?"

"We'd lose our insurance. Right now my treatments are covered, but if anything changes . . ." Lisa shrugged. "She likes to buy lottery tickets. She thinks that if she could hit a jackpot, our lives would change for the better."

That didn't make any sense to Nathan. "Would it?"

"She wants to take me places and show me things. Sometimes she acts like I'm not sick at all." Lisa smiled tightly. "At least Charlie's a realist."

"But the tumor *could* shrink again. It could go away for another long long time, couldn't it?"

"That's what gambling is all about, isn't it? Playing the odds."

Nathan screwed up his courage and asked, "What are the odds?"

She didn't answer, only patted his cheek. "You want to play another video game? I can't let you think you're better than me with a joystick."

Nathan didn't like the way she changed the subject, but the discussion was over and she wouldn't return to it.

17

Classes resumed with the new year. Nathan dropped the job and concentrated on getting homework completed in order to spend more time with Lisa. Besides, his crisis with his mother was over. She lightened up when he brought home straight As for first semester, and he'd been more respectful of her concerns about him.

Lisa left Fuller's classroom each afternoon for only the first couple of weeks in the month. When she began to stay for the full class period, Nathan asked, "Is radiation over?"

"Over. Except for feeling tired. I think I could sleep for a week."

"How—" She shot him a cautionary look and he remembered her warning not to ask about it. "I have a right to know," he groused.

She arched a perfect eyebrow, spun on her heel and walked away. He stood in the hall feeling left out and angry. He loved her. She should tell him something. He considered going to Charlie but discarded the idea because he knew Lisa wouldn't like it if he did.

At the end of January, Fuller called Nathan up after class once the room had emptied. The teacher said, "The school system is doing a joint effort with all senior English and art departments. They want to compile and publish the best student work in the metropolitan area. To this end, they're asking teachers in these disciplines to submit the best of their best student efforts." He steepled his fingers together. "I would very much like to submit the poem you wrote last semester. Is that all right?"

Nathan's jaw dropped. "*My* poem?"

Fuller riffled through a folder. "This one."

Nathan glanced at the paper, but naturally, he knew the words by heart. "I—I guess it's okay. Is it really good?"

"I wouldn't submit it if I didn't think so. Do you mind if I put your name on the work instead of your number?"

"I—I guess so." He stood as if rooted.

"Something else, Mr. Malone?"

"Did you pick others from our class?"

"Three others."

"How about the poem about Icarus? I never forgot that one."

"Why is that your concern, son?"

Nathan felt his face redden. "It isn't. I—I've just always wondered about the writer."

"It doesn't matter," Fuller said, straightening the folder. "The student won't give permission for the work to be submitted."

"You should come to the Valentine's dance with me." Nathan said the words lightly, right after he and Lisa had completed a game of Ping-Pong in his garage.

"Why should I do that?"

"Because I asked you to."

Lisa tossed the paddle on the table, slipped on her jacket. "That's sweet of you, but I hate school dances." She started for her cycle, parked in the driveway.

He caught her arm. "Skeet wants to take Jodie. They need wheels. I thought we could double."

"Can't you loan him your car?"

"Not without you and me in it."

She struggled not to grin. "So going to the dance would be a rescue mission? For Skeet and Jodie?"

"Pretty much." Nathan's heart hammered. He wanted to hold her and kiss her beautiful mouth.

"Well, since you put it like that." She threw her leg over her Harley.

"It's a date?" His heart was doing cartwheels.

"It's a date."

The Valentine's dance was held at one of Atlanta's posh country clubs. Nathan had looked forward to it for days and had rented a tux, bought Lisa a corsage, washed and waxed his car. When he and Skeet arrived at the apartment complex, Skeet hurried off to get Jodie, and Nathan went to Lisa's. She opened the door herself and Nathan gave a low whistle. She wore a long gown of midnight blue that shimmered when she moved. Her hair hung loose, not piled in fancy curls and sprayed stiff. "You're staring. This look all right?" she asked.

"I have no words."

Her features softened. "I'll report that to the saleslady."

"Where're Charlie and your mother?" Nathan realized Lisa was alone. *His* mother had taken a ton of photos before he could step out the door, plus given him a disposable camera with instructions to get shots of himself and his friends at the dance.

"They took a few days off and went to the casinos at Cherokee. A little vacation. Because it's Valentine's Day, Mom said she felt lucky."

He could tell that Lisa wasn't happy about the trip. "I feel lucky too. I'm with you," he said.

When they stepped into the main ballroom, heads swiveled and people whispered at the sight of them.

Jodie clung to Skeet. "Why is it that I can sing to a hundred strangers, but I can hardly walk into this room with kids I've gone to school with for years without breaking into a cold sweat?"

"If you did start singing, they'd fall at your feet," Skeet said.

"I miss our band," Jodie said with a sigh.

Larry had dropped them in favor of drumming for a rock group.

"We'll reorganize," Skeet told her.

But Nathan knew they wouldn't. Every free minute he had, he wanted to spend with Lisa. The band was a distant third behind Lisa and keeping his grades up. He had been applying to colleges, and in March he'd sit for the SATs again. He'd done fine on the test in October, but now he might do better. And better could mean a scholarship and going away to college.

The four of them found an empty table. "Punch?" Skeet asked. He left and returned minutes later balancing four cups. He set them on the table, looked about covertly, reached into his pocket and pulled out a half pint of whiskey. "Want some? I took it from the old man's stash."

Nathan sidled Lisa a glance. He didn't want to drink, but he would if she did.

Lisa shook her head. "Not tonight."

Relieved, Nathan turned down Skeet's offer too. Skeet looked disappointed. "You two aren't much fun."

"We're a lot of fun," Lisa said, patting his hand. "Jodie, get this guy dancing before he gets too loaded." Once they were alone, she asked Nathan, "Are you going to ask me to dance?"

"I can only dance to the slow ones," he confessed, remembering how she had danced at the frat party. "The other kind of dancing wasn't on my home-schooling schedule."

As soon as the music slowed, they went out onto the crowded floor. From the moment he took her in his arms, Nathan was certain he wouldn't be able to let go when the music stopped. Her perfume, a mixture of some spring flower and fresh rain, intoxicated him. The curve of her waist under his hand made him lightheaded. Her cheek rested on his shoulder, sending shivers straight through him, turning him clumsy and oafish.

Without warning, he felt a bump and turned to see the faces of Roddy and his date, a cheerleader named Crissy. "Whoops," Roddy said, without a hint of regret. Then he did a double-take as he looked from Nathan to Lisa.

Quickly Nathan ducked Lisa between two other couples, putting distance between them and the scowling Roddy. Nathan felt on top of the world. "Did you see the look on Rod's face? Now I know how Neanderthals felt when one brought home the biggest mastodon," he crowed in Lisa's ear.

She stopped dancing. "Are you comparing me to an extinct furry elephant?"

"No, no. I—I just meant—"

She burst out laughing. "I wish you could see *your* face, Malone."

He pulled her closer. "What I meant to say, he can't figure out how a babe like you would be seen with a doofus like me."

"Good recovery. But you're not a doofus," she said. "A dork, maybe, but no doofus."

"Thank you for raising my social status. I was really worried."

She laughed and it sounded like music.

By the time the dance was over and they'd stopped for coffee and arrived back at the apartment complex, Nathan was high on his own adrenaline, hating for the evening to be over, ever mindful of the curfew his mother had imposed. The notion of it brought him down. Skeet was feeling no pain, and once Nathan had parked and Skeet had exited the car with Jodie, Skeet said, "I'm going to crash on Jodie's sofa. Her mom will let me. I can't go home like this because the old man will kill me."

"He won't care if you're gone all night?"

"Get real. He keeps wishing I'd disappear."

Jodie steadied him, and Nathan watched them walk away.

"Come on," Lisa said, taking Nathan into her place. She kicked off her strappy high heels as she walked in the door. "Want a soda?"

"Sure." Suddenly, he didn't care about his stupid curfew. He was with Lisa, and that's where he wanted to be.

She poured them both a soda, gathered up the hem of her dress and retreated to her room. Nathan followed hesitantly. She flopped onto her bed, resting on her elbows, the long dress clinging to her every curve. He stood awkwardly at the door. She patted the bed. "I won't bite."

He sat next to her. "Well, fair warning: I *might*."

She studied him thoughtfully. "Thank you for tonight."

"That's my line."

"It gave me something I've always wanted."

"What's that?"

"Normal." Her expression had gone soft and serious. "Tonight I was a normal high school girl, going to a normal high school dance with three normal high school friends. I really had a good time."

He set down his drink, scooted closer to her. "I've never done it before either. I'm glad we got to do it with each other." He tucked her hair over her shoulder. "Lisa, I—"

She moved away from him, toward the headboard. "Are you going to get sentimental on me, Malone?"

He moved next to her. "Yes." He took her in his arms, kissed her mouth. She tasted of cold cola and cherry lip gloss and it made his head swim. When the kiss broke, he saw that her cheeks were damp. "Are you crying?" It wasn't the result he had hoped for.

She swiped her cheek, laughed self-consciously. "It's the sweetness of it all. You have no idea how wonderfully and terribly sweet this is to me. Sweet and normal."

He was confused because her emotions seemed all over the place—one minute joking, the next crying. Girls were baffling. "What can I say? I want to make you happy."

"Really?"

"I wouldn't have said it if I didn't mean it."

Tears pooled in her eyes. "I don't want you to leave," she said softly. "I don't want to be left alone."

His heart hammered as he realized how alone they were. The idea of staying made him lightheaded. He cupped her face, stared deeply into her violet eyes, and there he saw something else he'd never seen before. Her bravado was stripped away. He saw fear and loneliness. He saw pain and raw need. Her walls were down, and he knew he couldn't leave her. "Let me make a call," he told her.

He went into the hall and with shaking fingers punched in his home number. His mother answered on the second ring. "Mom?"

"Are you all right?"

"Mom, I'm fine."

"What's wrong?"

"Nothing's wrong. I'm going to be late, that's all."

"How late will you be?"

He took a deep breath. "I'll be home in the morning, first thing."

"You'll *what*? You have no permission—"

"Mom, don't."

"You don't call me and announce that you're staying out all night! Where are you anyway?"

"I'm safe. I—I'm with Lisa."

"Where are her parents?"

His mother was too insightful, for he'd hoped he wouldn't have to tell her everything until the next day. Still, he wasn't going to lie to her either. "They're not here."

Dead silence, then, "Have you been drinking?"

"Not a drop. Let me talk to Dad."

When his father came on the line, Nathan said, "I'm calling because I don't want Mom calling the police. I'm safe, sober, and sane. I know what I'm doing. Trust me. Please."

His mother came back on the phone. "This is ridiculous, Nathan. You can't—"

"But I am. I'll be home in a few hours."

"That girl is poison!"

"Mom . . . I love you." He cut off the call, turned off his cell phone and flipped it closed. He went back into the room to be with Lisa.

18

The next morning Lisa surprised him by coming to his house with him. "You don't have to," he said. "Yes, I do."

They rode in silence and walked into the kitchen hand in hand. His parents were at the table, his father flipping through the newspaper, his mother feeding the twins. Karen looked up, and her angry expression gave way to one of surprise. The twins squealed when they saw Nathan and Lisa. Karen returned to feeding them cereal and bananas. "Sit down until I finish with the girls," she said.

Nathan first poured himself and Lisa cups of coffee. He nodded at his father, who raised his eyebrows and returned to his paper. The tension in the room was like summer air before a rainstorm, thick and oppressive, and except for the burbling of Audrey and Abby, no one spoke. When the girls were finished eating, Karen washed them up and carried them to their playpen in the other room, where they could be seen from the doorway. The moment she stepped back into the kitchen, Lisa said, "It was my fault Nathan didn't come home last night. He did it as a favor to me because I asked him to."

Karen was in no mood for either excuses or apologies. "I know you both think my rules are old-fashioned and provincial. I know you both believe that enlightened parents let their kids make the rules. I know you have freedoms that Nathan doesn't have, Lisa. But common sense dictates that rules and safeguards are for a person's protection, not simply an annoyance to be circumvented any way possible."

Nathan knew she was just getting warmed up.

"What are you two *thinking*? Spending the night together? Do you believe I'm so stupid as to not remember teenage hormones? For god's sake, what if you got pregnant? You'd ruin both your lives!"

Nathan felt heated embarrassment and anger over his mother's tirade. He wanted to yell back at her, but Lisa spoke first, her voice calm, quiet. "That won't happen, Mrs. Malone. I won't get pregnant because, you see, I won't live long enough to ever have a baby."

She went on to tell Nathan's parents everything about her tumor, much as she'd told Nathan. Her voice was soft, her eyes dry, as if the fear and pain she'd felt last night in her room had vanished with the rising of the sun. At some point, his mother sat down at the table, her face a mask of disbelief. "And now the second round of radiation is over," Lisa said. "Unfortunately it hasn't helped much. The tumor hasn't shrunk, but at least it's dormant. We don't know for how long."

This was news to Nathan, and he felt as if he'd been punched.

"They want to try a new kind of Gamma Knife radiation, but it's a long shot too. The tumor's just too close to some vital brain tissue."

"Are you going to do it anyway?" Nathan's question turned Lisa's attention his way.

"I want to graduate. A person needs goals and that's mine. So if I do it, it won't be until after school's over." She looked again at Karen and Craig. "I swore Nathan to secrecy, made him promise to tell no one what was happening to me. He kept that promise and I hope you won't hold it against him. It's my story. My life. Please . . . don't . . . punish him."

From the other room, Audrey wailed because Abby had bopped her on the head with a plastic block. Karen pushed herself up from the table with both hands, wavered for a moment as if she were shouldering a heavy weight. "I—I have to think about this, Lisa."

"I understand."

She paused at the doorway, her back to them. "I— I'm sorry that you're sick."

"So am I," Lisa said.

Nathan's father cleared his throat. "Thank you for telling us."

"You needed to know."

Karen said, "I had a daughter once and lost her."

"Nathan told me."

"I miss her every day."

Nathan caught sight of Molly's old drawing still stuck to the refrigerator across the room. The drawing had been laminated. A lump formed in his throat that he could not swallow.

Oddly, Nathan's family did not talk about Lisa's illness at his house, and the incident of his staying out all night melted away. He ran into Lisa's mother and Charlie whenever he went over to get Lisa, and they were friendly to him. "You're such a nice young man," Jill would tell him if she was home. "I told Lisa she should find a nice guy and leave those losers behind."

Nathan was hesitant to hear more about "those losers." There were some things he didn't want to know.

Charlie always greeted him with a smile and a handshake. "You've settled our girl down . . . something I've been trying to do for years," he told Nathan one time.

"I'm thinking of pulling the plugs from her cycle and then she'll depend on me one hundred percent."

That made Charlie laugh. "It's a plan."

In the following weeks, Lisa came over more often, and by mid-March on a sunny Saturday morning she actually helped Nathan and his mother replant pansies in the flower beds. Karen pulled up the limp and wasted plants, hit hard by winter, and Nathan dug small holes for Lisa, who plucked fresh plants from a flat of multicolored flowers and poked them into the prepared ground. "You sure you want to do this?" he asked during a break. His mother had gone inside to make a pitcher of lemonade because the spring day had turned hot.

"I like doing it. It makes me feel good to know that something beautiful will grow because I planted it."

"They're just pansies. We'll rip them out in May and June and plant hot-weather flowers."

"So? They're pretty now." She examined one closely, puffed a breath onto fragile lavender flower petals. "I think these are my favorites. The color's perfect." She glanced over at him. "Why are you smiling?"

"Just remembering that girl on the motorcycle who used to blow me off. You're not so tough."

"And you're not so nerdy."

"Is that what you thought of me?"

She gave him a look of pure innocence. "That's my secret."

He grinned, decided to ask her what had been on his mind for weeks. "How come you won't let Fuller submit your pieces in that countywide student works book?"

"I wasn't asked." They were sitting on the ground, and she grabbed her knees and pulled them against her chest.

"Sure you were. You're number four-five-four."

"Who told you that?"

"No one told me. I just know that you are. The poem about flying into the sun—I liked it a lot. You wrote it, didn't you?"

"I've always wanted to fly. Yes, I wrote it."

He was elated because he had figured out her identity. "I *knew* it was you."

He also knew that her poem was a metaphor for death. He got it, but just as he had learned not to ask questions about her health, he didn't bring it up. "Submissions don't close until next week. You should let Fuller submit it."

"Did you tell him he could use yours? You know, the one about loving someone from afar?"

He grinned sheepishly—no use denying it now. "How long have you known?"

"Since the day he first read it. You really do wear your heart in your eyes, Malone."

"A turnoff?"

In answer, she leaned forward and kissed his mouth.

"Hey, Nate, Lisa, wait up."

Nathan and Lisa turned at the sound of their names in the hallway as they were leaving school. Skeet and Jodie were heading straight at them. "What's up?"

"Have you heard about Roddy?"

"Don't think so. What's happened?"

"He's flunking and won't walk for graduation." Skeet sounded downright gleeful.

"He has to go to summer school, and a lot of college coaches have backed off from scholarship offers," Jodie added. "I guess the term *dumb jock* really applies, huh?"

"He could have studied," Lisa said. "He thought he could coast because he could play ball."

"Couldn't happen to a nicer guy," Skeet said.

"You're getting far too much pleasure out of this, my man," Nathan said, grinning.

"It's been a long time coming." Skeet chuckled. "Hey, prom's next month, and I think we should all go together."

Nathan hadn't broached the subject with Lisa yet, although he assumed that they would be going. He still wasn't a hundred percent sure of her. She was moody and could retreat into her own world without warning. "I agree. What do you say?"

"You drinking again?" Lisa asked Skeet.

Skeet made a face. "No way. I was hungover for two days."

"Prom *is* a rite of passage," Nathan reminded Lisa.

"A new adventure," Jodie said, looking hopeful. "And it wouldn't be the same without the two of you."

"Plus," Skeet said with a covert glance around, "it'll be a sort of celebration. Come April, I'll be eighteen and I'm moving into my own place."

"What are you talking about?" This was the first Nathan had heard of this.

"Larry and two other guys rent an apartment together and one of the guys is moving out. Larry asked me if I wanted to move in and I jumped at the chance."

"It makes sense," Jodie said. "You know how his stepfather treats him."

"How're you going to pay for it?" Nathan asked, taken aback by Skeet's announcement. There was a time when Skeet told him everything first.

"I've got money saved. And as soon as school's out, I'll get a car. My mom said she'd get me one if I graduated. Then I'm starting into the management training program at the grocery store. My supervisor asked me if I wanted to. He said I had 'potential.' Think of it! Winston George Andrews has potential."

"What about college?"

"You're college material, Nate, not me." Skeet slapped him on the shoulder. "This is a cool move, man. I'll be living on my own *and* collecting a full-time paycheck."

"I'm glad for you," Lisa said.

"So that's why prom is even more of an event. We'll be celebrating the start of my new life."

"A worthy cause," Lisa said, her eyes bright with an inner light only Nathan saw.

In late March, Lisa told Nathan that she would be out of classes for a week. "For some tests," she said vaguely. "I'll call you when I surface."

Grateful that she'd told him that much, he hunkered down and missed her like crazy. By the following Saturday, he hadn't heard from her. He called her cell number, only to have some voice announce that the number was no longer in service. She hadn't told him she was planning on getting a new cell number either.

He grabbed his car keys and told his mother, "I'm heading over to Lisa's."

At the complex, Nathan wove around to the back, parked in an available space, and jogged toward her apartment. The door was open, and when he stepped inside, he was greeted by two handymen in coveralls. A carpet steaming machine stood near freshly painted drywall. Otherwise, the place was empty.

"Can I help you?" one of the painters asked.

"The people who live here . . . where are they?" His heart hammered and he felt cold all over. *Where is she?*

"I guess they've moved, buddy. We get called in to repaint and clean the carpets after a tenant goes. According to the front office manager, there's been nobody here for almost a week now."

19

*N*athan skirted the painters and went straight to Lisa's room, where only blank walls and hollow echoes greeted him. The mural of the flame trees had been partially ripped from the wall and lay in shreds on the carpet like shed skin. He bent and retrieved a swatch, turned it over to see the bright blossoms, and remembered how Lisa's hands had caressed the paper the night of the dance. A million dreams ago.

He wadded the paper, threw it at the wall and left. He jogged across the parking lot to the front office, where he burst inside, startling the woman behind the front desk. "The people in 5193, Charlie Terry and his family . . . where are they?"

The woman sized him up. "Calm down, young man." She picked up a clipboard, turned several sheets of paper, ran her finger down a column, looked up. "They've moved."

He gritted his teeth. "Where?"

"Even if I had that information—which I don't—laws prohibit me from revealing it."

"They didn't tell you *anything*?"

She sighed. "Mr. Terry simply came in last week and said they were leaving."

"There must be a forwarding address! A phone number!"

"No, there isn't. Mr. Terry said that he'd notify us as to where to mail his deposits. Which he may not get back since he failed to give our customary two weeks' notice."

"But—but . . ."

"I'm sorry," the woman said. "I have no other information for you. You'd best run along now."

"If—if Charlie calls, will you ask him to *please* contact Nathan?"

"I'm not a message service."

"Please!"

She agreed, but Nathan saw by her expression that as soon as he was out the door, she'd forget his name.

Nathan went to Jodie's apartment and pounded on the door. Jodie opened it, took one look at Nathan and asked, "What's wrong?"

"Where's Lisa gone?"

Skeet padded up behind Jodie in bare feet. "Hey, man."

"Lisa's gone? I—I didn't know," Jodie said, peeking

out the door and toward Lisa's apartment. "Lisa's gone," she said over her shoulder to Skeet.

"But you live just down the parking lot from her! All her furniture is out. They're repainting. She's moved. How can you not know?"

"Hey, Jodie says she doesn't know. Don't be in her face," Skeet said.

Jodie tugged at Skeet's arm. "He didn't mean anything by it." She turned back to Nathan. "I swear, I don't know. I'm in school all day and Mom works. I didn't see a trailer or moving van when I *was* home."

"But you're her friend!"

"She often doesn't call me, especially now that Skeet and me are together. You know how she is, she keeps to herself a lot."

Nathan slumped against the doorjamb. "Why would she do this? Why would she leave without telling me?"

"Oh, Nathan, I'm so sorry!" The words came from his mother. "And you had no idea they'd just pick up and go?"

"Lisa told me she had to go through some tests."

"Maybe the test results showed something that needed immediate attention."

Nathan didn't find comfort in that thought. "But why wouldn't she say something to me? Why would she and her family sneak out of town? All their cell phone numbers don't work, and they left no way to reach them."

Karen lifted Abby from a changing table and handed her to Nathan. She picked up Audrey and laid her on the table, fetching a paper diaper from a shelf below. "She's a very independent girl, Nathan. She doesn't think or act like you do."

"What's that supposed to mean?" Abby tried to grab his lower lip.

"Don't get defensive. I've actually come to like the girl. But she *is* different. You must admit that."

"Different isn't a bad thing." His mother's analysis annoyed him.

"No, but different is, well, *different.* She plays by different rules, guards her privacy like a junkyard dog, and has never made you any promises that you've talked about. Which leads me to think she understands her dilemma and purposefully doesn't form attachments."

The truths were too much for Nathan. Lisa had made him no promises. *He* was the one who had made them. *He* was the one who had pledged his undying love and tried with all his heart to keep and protect her. And now she had vanished. "She shouldn't have left this way," he said, more hurt than angry.

"I agree," his mother said. "But remember, people have reasons for making the choices they do, and although we don't understand them, we must accept them."

"But how will I know how she's doing? How will I know when she gets really sick?"

His mother relieved him of Abby and, balancing each baby on a hip, said, "That is the worst part, Nate . . . the not knowing. I've wondered thousands of times if Molly cried for me to rescue her from the water. I don't know. I'll never know."

He saw emotional pain etched in her face just before she turned and carried the twins downstairs. He felt for her, and for himself, both now united by grief.

Nathan couldn't concentrate at school, and after a week he considered asking his mother to supervise him for the final two months of high school. The twins were older and maybe she could handle his schooling like before. Maybe he could even test out and receive his diploma in the mail. Crestwater was just a big, indifferent institution as far as Nathan was concerned, and he wanted out. Certainly except for himself, Skeet and Jodie, no one seemed to notice that Lisa wasn't there. "She came and went a lot," Jodie told him. "People got used to it."

"And she didn't exactly go out of her way to make friends," Skeet said.

Those things didn't matter to Nathan. Lisa was gone and there was a hole in his life large enough to walk through. Even his guitars brought him no comfort. His music had dried up. He felt empty of song.

Fuller called Nathan up to his desk before Easter break. The final bell had sounded, the room had cleared, and in his raspy voice he said, "I wanted to tell you that your poem has been selected for the countywide book that will be published in the fall. Congratulations."

There was a time when the news would have elated Nathan. Now it was just information.

"The competition was stiff," Fuller went on to say. "Thousands of entries, but only two hundred chosen, plus sixty-five student art projects. Nice job, Mr. Malone."

"Were any others picked from Crestwater?"

"One more. At the last minute, student four-five-four allowed me to also submit their work, which surprised me. I'd thought persuading this student was a lost cause."

"The Icarus poem."

"That was the one. How did you know?"

"I asked the author about it, and she told me she had written it, and I told her she should let you submit it."

"So then you know everything?"

"Yes." Nathan's gaze held Fuller's. "I don't suppose you know what happened to the author, do you?"

"Sadly, no. The only message a teacher gets from the administration is that a student will no longer be in class and has left our area." He shook his head. "Pity. She was quite gifted."

Nathan's brief flare of hope that Fuller might know something about Lisa's whereabouts dimmed. "Thanks," he said dully.

"Mr. Malone, *you* too are talented. Also, you're a good student, and if you ever need faculty recommendations on college applications, I'll be glad to write one for you."

"Thanks again." Nathan scooped up his books and went to the door.

"You aren't alone in missing student four-five-four, Mr. Malone."

Skeet and Jodie hung with Nathan over the break and worked hard to raise his spirits. They were playing a video game in his basement one morning when Jodie asked, "Do you know why Lisa was so secretive about her personal life? I've always wondered."

"She never told you anything?" This surprised Nathan because he figured girls shared every morsel of information they possessed.

"Do you know something?"

Now that Lisa had fled, there was no reason to keep her secret. It might also help his two friends realize that his sense of loss wasn't just the pinings of a lovesick puppy. He set down his game controller and without any buildup told them all he'd known for the past many months. Jodie's expression turned to shock, then she cried. "Cancer? Lisa has brain cancer?"

Skeet went slack-jawed. "Get out."

"It's true. All those months she skipped out of last period, she was going for radiation treatments."

"I—I remember she'd sometimes get headaches," Jodie said, blowing her nose. "She told me they were migraines."

"Much worse," Nathan said.

"So I guess she got worse?" Skeet ventured.

"The first question I'll ask, if I can track her down before . . ." He couldn't finish the sentence.

Jodie said, "Tell me again how you've tried to find her."

Nathan went down his list. "All dead ends."

"Did you go to the construction company where Charlie and her mom worked?"

Nathan sat upright. "No. I didn't."

"People get final paychecks. If they left quickly, the place may have a way to reach them."

"You're a genius!" Nathan jumped up, renewed hope surging through him, followed swiftly by disappointment. "I don't know where they worked."

"I do," Jodie said.

"Let's go."

"Wait a minute," Jodie said. "I have an idea, so let me handle this. Besides, I think a curious friendly girlfriend trumps a desperate hysterical boyfriend in this instance."

Eventually they drove to the site where Jodie knew Lisa's mother had last worked, and parked across the street. Before Nathan and Skeet could get out of the car, Jodie stopped them. "Sit. It's best I go alone."

"But—" Nathan started.

"Tie him up if you have to," she told Skeet. Taking her purse and a shopping bag, she crossed the street and entered the construction trailer.

Time dragged and Nathan thought he'd jump out of his skin from the suspense. "What's taking so long?"

"It's only been fifteen minutes, dude. She'll come through," Skeet said. "This girl's outstanding."

It seemed as if an eternity had passed before Jodie emerged from the trailer and came back across the street. She scooted into the backseat.

"Well?" Nathan demanded. "Don't make me go postal."

Jodie grinned and handed him a folded slip of paper. "Charlie Terry's new cell phone number."

Nathan snatched it. "You did it, Jodie! Man, you're terrific!"

"I told you so!" Skeet reached around and hugged her. "How did you do it?"

"I went to the only woman in there. She's taken over Lisa's mother's job, and I said that I was Lisa's best friend and that she'd left before the yearbooks came out and that I *had* to make sure she got hers because it *is* her senior year . . . blah-blah-blah." She pulled a book from her bag and grinned. "I cried too. Real tears."

"Brilliant," Skeet stated. "Especially since new yearbooks aren't even out yet."

"Last year's edition was a convincing prop. I just waved it around and she never got too close a look at it."

"Did she say where they've moved?" Nathan asked, staring at the cell number and committing it to memory.

"Someplace in Miami," Jodie said. "You'll have to get Charlie to tell you where."

20

$\mathcal{N}$ athan waited until he was alone to make the call on his cell phone. Charlie answered on the second ring.

"It's me, Charlie. It's Nathan Malone. Please don't hang up."

After a pause, Charlie's soft drawl came through. "I knew you were resourceful, son. How did you find us?"

"From where you used to work," Nathan told him.

Charlie chuckled. "I told Lisa that it was a mistake for her not to tell you we were leaving. I said you'd figure out something."

"H-how is she?"

"Bad."

Nathan felt his stomach heave. "I want to see her."

"She doesn't want you to see her like this—the way

she is now. You know how she gets when she digs in her heels."

"I know, and I don't care. Please tell me where you are. I'm coming."

"We're in Miami. That's a good ten-hour drive from Atlanta."

"So?"

"Your parents might not like it."

"I'm coming," Nathan repeated, knowing he had one monster of a fight in front of him.

That evening after the twins were in bed, Nathan packed a duffel bag. He went down to the kitchen, stood in the doorway, watched his mother roll out pastry dough and gathered his courage. At the table, his father sat fiddling with his laptop. Nathan wondered why he hadn't noticed this about the two of them before—they liked being in the same room with each other, even if they were doing different things. *Togetherness.* He had wanted that with Lisa.

Nathan stepped into the lighted room. "Mom, Dad . . . I've found Lisa. I just talked to Charlie and he told me where they are in Miami."

Both his parents turned his way. Karen said, "That's a relief. How is she doing?"

"Not so good."

His father shook his head. "That's too bad. I'm sorry."

"I want to go and see her."

"When?" Craig asked.

"As soon as possible. I could leave in the morning."

"Tomorrow's a school day."

"I don't care."

"You've just come off spring break," Karen said. "You still have six weeks of school left. You can't just pick up and leave."

"I haven't taken a single sick day this year. My grades are perfect. I can afford to take the time."

"Well, I can't," Karen said. "I can't just drop everything and go with you. And neither can your father. Have you thought about trying to drive all that way with the girls?"

"I'm not asking you to go."

It took a second for his statement to sink in, and when it did, his mother declared, "Well, you can't go by yourself."

"Why not?"

"Oh, Nathan, let's not have an argument. You can't go to Miami alone. You don't know a soul there and you have no place to stay. It's unrealistic to expect Lisa's family to take you in."

"I wouldn't even ask them. They're living in a motel while Lisa's in this special facility."

His mother returned to her pastry project. "No, son. You aren't going."

He walked over to the counter where she stood, removed the rolling pin, guided his mother to a chair, sat her down and crouched in front of her. Holding both her hands in his, he said, "She's dying, Mom."

"I—I understand that, but—"

"Let me ask you something," he interrupted. "What would you give if you could spend one more day with Molly? Just one?"

Tears welled in Karen's eyes. "That's not fair."

"I have a chance to see Lisa one more time. Please don't try to take it away from me."

"Karen." They both glanced at Nathan's father, who had spoken. "Let him go."

Tears spilled onto Karen's cheeks. "But—"

Craig held up his hand. "I'll call my old boss, Bernie Steadman. He and his family live near Miami now and I know they'll let Nathan stay with them. Our son will be all right. And he should have the opportunity to do this."

Nathan hadn't expected his dad's support, but he was grateful.

Karen pulled away, wiped her cheeks. Her shoulders slumped, but Nathan knew she had capitulated. "You'll call every few hours?"

Nathan rose. "Twice a day. I promise."

"What if—?"

"I'll be fine, Mom. Really."

"How long will you stay?"

"For as long as she'll let me be with her."

The Sisters of Mercy, a Respite and Haven for the Terminally Ill, was an amazingly beautiful facility set on several acres in Coral Gables, Florida, a suburb of Miami. Nathan drove slowly along the driveway, which was sheltered by banyan trees, palms, and palmettos and bordered by brilliantly hued flowering hibiscus bushes and bougainvillea vines of hot fuchsia pink. It seemed that he was off in a tropical wilderness instead of near a city. The main building where he was scheduled to meet Charlie looked like a Spanish hacienda crowned with red barrel roof tiles. With its cream-colored stucco walls, decorative wrought iron, large wooden beams overhead and red-clay Spanish tile underfoot, the place looked more like a resort than a hospital. Yet it *was* a hospital— one that specialized in caring for the dying.

The lobby was peppered with groupings of sofas and comfy chairs. A nun, in a crisp short white dress, a pale blue apron, and a starched white head covering, sat behind a carved desk of darkest wood. A simple wooden cross hung around her neck. "May I help you?"

Before he could answer, he heard his name called from across the lobby. He looked up to see Charlie and Jill, heading toward him. Charlie shook his hand, then showed him to a side porch, where people sat visiting patients around bamboo tables. Ceiling fans moved the perfumed tropical air.

"Aren't you a sight for sore eyes," Jill said, with a big smile. "Are you settled in?"

"Yes, with a friend of my dad's over on Key Biscayne." Now that he was actually here, Nathan felt nervous and anxious. It had been weeks since he'd seen Lisa, and he didn't know what to expect. "This is a nice place," he said, glancing around.

Jill beamed a smile. "We want my baby to have the best. We don't do the Catholic thing, but the sisters here know that. They're real kind to everybody. There's a waiting list, but Lisa's doctor at Emory made the arrangements and we're real grateful. I just couldn't stand to think about my little girl stuck in that apartment in Atlanta, or some pathetic nursing home. She always liked Miami, you know. So this is where we brought her."

"Does Lisa know I'm here?" Nathan asked.

"She didn't want you to come at first," Charlie said.

"If you changed her mind, thank you."

Charlie chuckled. "I didn't exactly, but I did tell her I thought it was the *nice* thing to do."

Jill said, "It's not that Lisa doesn't care about you. It's just . . . just that things are so bad for her. She wanted you to remember her the way she was."

"When can I see her?"

"She's outside in the courtyard, under that big tree."

Nathan saw her then through the screen. She sat in a wheelchair, a throw across her lap, shadows and sunlight sprinkling through lacy leaves of a single great tree that spread umbrella-like over the entire stone courtyard. The tree blazed with red blossoms, like a living fire. *A flame tree.*

He walked to the screen door and Charlie walked with him. "A few things you need to know before you go out there," Charlie said. "They shaved her head for the Gamma Knife procedure that didn't work."

"Hair doesn't matter to me," Nathan said.

"And one more thing," Charlie said. "She's blind."

At the sound of his approach, Lisa turned toward him. She only had sounds to guide her now, but she was getting good at distinguishing between approaching nuns and others. "Hello, Malone."

Nathan halted in front of her chair, a knot in his throat so big that he couldn't speak right away. She looked small and thin, fragile in the chair, her shorn head covered by a silk scarf. All the frustration and resentment he'd been nursing since she'd left without a word to him evaporated.

"So, do you like my new look?" she asked. "I've heard that bald is in."

He stooped, took her hands. "You're beautiful."

"Liar."

"I love you."

She stiffened. "Why did you come?"

"To tell you that."

She sighed, turned her face aside. "I wanted to crawl off and die alone. I thought it was the best thing."

"Not for me. I want to be with you."

"Don't make this any harder, Malone."

He sat on the cool gray stones at the foot of her chair. "Jodie and Skeet say hello. Mom and Dad say that they miss you. Fuller says both our poems made the cut for the best of Atlanta student works book. The twins are standing up on their own now. We missed the prom."

"The twins are standing?" Lisa ignored the other announcements.

"They walk around holding on to furniture. They fall a lot, but they keep getting up and doing it again. They're pretty cute. For girls."

Lisa smiled, imagining the babies in her mind's eye. "How are Charlie and my mom doing?"

"They're sad, but they're okay."

"Good. I wish . . ." She didn't finish, but reached out. He leaned into her touch, and her fingers followed the contours of his face and then his hair. "Your hair's longer."

"No time to get it cut." His voice almost broke.

"I miss riding my cycle," she said wistfully. "I loved the sense of freedom it gave me."

"Remember that party when I climbed on the back and wouldn't get off?"

"We talked for an hour at that bookstore."

"I thought you were bored."

"I thought you just wanted bragging rights—you know, locker-room talk about how you bagged Lisa Lindstrom for a night."

"If I could have lived in your back pocket, I would have."

"I'm sorry about that frat party."

He shrugged, realized she couldn't see his movement. "I was crazy jealous. I couldn't stand it. I hated every guy you'd ever been with."

"That night you stayed with me, after the Valentine's dance—"

"A highlight of my life." He smoothed her lap blanket. "You regret it?"

"Not at all."

His heart skipped a beat. "I loved you more, if that's possible." He saw moisture fill her sightless eyes. "Lisa, I'm glad you got to come here . . . to this place."

She smiled. "When I first came, I could still see, and when I saw this tree, I knew it was where I wanted to be. Isn't it beautiful?"

"Beautiful," he said, without taking his eyes off her.

She took a deep breath and he heard her weariness in it. "I should go back to my room. I don't want to embarrass myself by falling out of my chair out here. Tell Charlie when you go inside."

"I'll send him out." Nathan wasn't ready to leave. He never wanted to leave her, yet he got up slowly. She was shutting down and he understood that he must respect her privacy. "Thank you for letting me come."

"Did I have a choice? You're a very persistent guy, Malone." Her smile lingered.

"A favor?"

"What?"

"Say my first name. You never call me by my first name."

"Nathan."

From her lips, it sounded like a prayer. He rocked back on his heels, struggling not to cry.

She said, "We had a great ride, didn't we?"

He bent and kissed her lips quickly before she could pull away. "We had a great ride."

He cautiously stepped backward, keeping her in his sight as long as possible. A breeze stirred the air and the towering flame tree above her. A shower of tiny red petals fluttered down, twirling and falling to bathe her in a thousand flashes of pure crimson.

She felt them fall, lifted her face toward the sky and caught them on her cheeks, eyelids, soft lips.

Sunlight and shadow flicked over her, reminding Nathan of Spanish lace entwined with tears of brightest red.

She raised her arms, caught drifting petals in her lap and upturned palms; she was Icarus ready to touch the sun.

Nine days later, on a warm Thursday morning when he rolled out of bed to face another day of his waning hours of high school, Nathan picked up his cell phone to stuff it in his backpack. He flipped it open to check on battery life and saw that he had a text message. His heart thudded and his fingers went cold and numb. Still, he punched in the code to access the message. In abbreviated form, it read:

"Lisa took flight 3:09 this morning. Charlie"

21

athan pushed the wheelbarrow across the backyard while balancing the tree it carried. The twins squealed as he passed them. They were contained inside their baby corral, a sturdy plastic fence that encircled most of the surface of the patio. The corral was heaped with toys, but Abby wanted out and let him know it.

"I'm busy, Ab," he told her, even though she couldn't understand. Audrey pulled herself up beside her sister and joined the clamor.

"They want you to play with them," his mother said. "They adore their big brother." She'd been weeding the flower beds next to the patio. She wiped her hands on a towel tied around her waist, and came toward him. "What kind of tree did you buy?"

Nathan set down the barrow. "A weeping willow."

"That's fitting," she said, with a sympathetic smile. "A good choice, son." His mother fingered the bright green foliage budding on the branches. "It will need full sun. And lots of space; they grow quite large."

"It's a dwarf variety."

"Smart thinking."

"So, where should I start digging?"

His mother scanned the yard. "I've really packed it in, haven't I? How about in the middle, maybe ten yards or so from the magnolia."

"Molly's magnolia?" He was surprised. That tree was practically sacred.

"Your tree for Lisa should have a place of honor," Karen said quietly.

He pushed the wheelbarrow to the middle of the yard, then counted off ten long paces from the great magnolia. It was dotted with cream-colored flowers, their heavy perfume filling the air. He took out a shovel and sank it into the hard red Georgia clay. Within minutes sweat was running off his body and blisters were forming on his palms. Every drop of sweat, every throb of his hands was for Lisa's sake, and he welcomed the pain.

School was out; graduation a memory. In another month, he'd be leaving for college—and leaving his boyhood behind forever. He'd accepted an academic scholarship to a small college in Kentucky that had offered him full tuition for his freshman year. It had come buoyed by his high SAT scores, good grades, and several letters of recommendation—the best one from Max Fuller. Kentucky was a good choice, he thought. Not too far away, but far enough. He needed a change of scenery.

"I'll help you dig," his mother said, coming up beside him.

"That's okay. You were right—it's something a person needs to do alone."

She nodded, looked toward the patio when Audrey let out a wail. Abby had thrown her own sippy cup over the side of the corral and had taken her sister's in consolation. His mom sighed. "I'd better go referee."

Nathan watched her cross the lawn and pick up Abby's cup. He chuckled, imagining how busy his mother was going to be with them over the years. He loved his little sisters, the only sisters he would ever know in the cycle of life. A cycle neither Molly nor Lisa had gotten to fulfill. He had thought a lot about Molly lately. Although he hadn't known her well, hardly remembered her, in fact, she had left a gaping wound in his family when she'd left. Just as Lisa had left a wound in his heart when she died.

Lisa had been one of a kind—secretive, hardheaded, independent, wild and daring, but also smart, witty, well read, a gifted writer, loyal to her friends, and kind to the underdogs of life. And she would always be his standard of measure for loving someone again.

The hole had grown deep and Nathan tossed down

the shovel. He loosened the dirt in the container holding the tree, and with both hands lifted it free of the bucket. He set it in the hole, picked up the shovel and began to fill in around the root-ball. Next he would water it thoroughly so that it could begin its own life cycle in his mother's gardens.

As he worked, from inside his head, and quite unexpectedly, music began to form, beautiful notes that needed his guitar for purest expression. The music drifted in and out, and he savored it. Then words formed, fragments of a song. What had Fuller said about good writing? *It comes from the heart, not the head.* And so he hummed while he waited for the new music to make the journey from his mind to his heart and into his soul.

Lurlene McDaniel began writing inspirational novels about teenagers facing life-altering situations when her son was diagnosed with juvenile diabetes. "I want kids to know that while people don't get to choose what life gives to them, they do get to choose how they respond."

Her many novels, which have received acclaim from readers, teachers, parents, and reviewers, are hard-hitting and realistic but also leave readers with inspiration and hope.

Lurlene McDaniel lives in Chattanooga, Tennessee.